# HEALING STICKS

*by*

Stephen John French

Please call

*[signature]* Stephen J. French 6-1-08

PublishAmerica

Baltimore

623-308-6346

First printing

ISBN: 1-4137-0923-0
PUBLISHED BY PUBLISHAMERICA, LLLP
www.publishamerica.com
Baltimore

Printed in the United States of America

This book is dedicated to my Lord Jesus who by His kindness and mercy brought me to a place in my life where I am able to live freely in great peace and joy for what He has done in my heart. In return I give my life and my love back to Him.

This book is also dedicated to my mother Margaret A. French and my older brother David Clayton French Jr. who went home to be with the Lord on December 6, 1995, at the age of 41.

# TABLE OF CONTENTS


CHAPTER 1
Healing Sticks . . . . . . . . . . . . . . . . . . . . . . . . . .7

CHAPTER 2
The Cross Revealed . . . . . . . . . . . . . . . . . .29

CHAPTER 3
The Precious Blood of Jesus . . . . . . . . . . . . . . .44

CHAPTER 4
A Carpenter's Dream . . . . . . . . . . . . . . . .56

CHAPTER 5
O Jerusalem, Jerusalem . . . . . . . . . . . . . . . . . .70

CHAPTER 6
False Prophets . . . . . . . . . . . . . . . . . . . . . . . .76

CHAPTER 7
Your Eyes are Doves . . . . . . . . . . . . . . . . . . . .94

CHAPTER 8
Walking and Leaping and Praising God . . . . . . .114

CHAPTER 9
He Who has an Ear Let Him Hear . . . . . . . . . . .127

CHAPTER 10
Behold, I Stand at the Door . . . . . . . . . . . . . . .139

TESTIMONY . . . . . . . . . . . . . . . . . . . . . . . . . . .165

NOTES . . . . . . . . . . . . . . . . . . . . . . . . . . . . . .167

# CHAPTER 1
# Healing Sticks

Everybody knew my name, for I was considered a great person. I was in the running for a well-known magazine's "Man of the Year" award and considered to be the front-runner for this prestigious distinction. Rumors were flying everywhere like a child's kite flipping wildly in the breeze and the only thing keeping it from destroying itself was a small string clutched tightly in a young boy's hand. I was that kite and my destiny was just as feeble as the string. Who would have ever believed it, I never felt I would get any prize, noble or not, because when reality set in I was just plain, old, ordinary me. My face had been plastered everywhere, on television, on the front covers of magazines, newscasts, and talk shows were all inflamed with the fire that had become my life. It seemed that I was more recognized than the President of the United States and to some, even more popular. I even had personal bodyguards dispatched to watch my home and follow me wherever I went, so in a way I guess my lifestyle was kind of presidential to a certain degree. My days were extremely long and exhausting, but sometimes they were exhilarating as well.

On this particular morning I was walking out my front door to go to yet another busy day of meetings. I closed the door and looked around as I usually do to see if my bodyguards were lurking around unseen as they were hired to do. As I turned walking towards my car, a man came running up near the driveway shaking a gun and demanding a stick as he shrieked out his orders in a hysterical crackling manner. I was too stunned to think quickly or feel any fear. The gunmen was about fifteen feet in front of me when he bellowed out in sheer panic, "Give me a stick or I'll shoot you!" he cried.

Forget what I said about fear because now I was shaking and I stammered back, "If you've read anything about me you know I don't carry any of the sticks with me!"

"I don't believe you!" he shouted back violently. Apparently he was as shaken and as frightened as I was. "Give me a stick or I'll shoot you and take it from you," he demanded.

He may have been delusional or momentarily insane and I could smell fear riveting out of him like a nuclear power plant with rising toxic fumes getting ready to rupture. "Please," I yelled back to him, "Don't, don't do anything foolish that you will regret."

His eyes seemed a blazed and brightly orange, demonic in nature as he aimed and fired the gun. Instinctively, I jumped as the bullet whizzed between my legs and I plunged to the ground falling in a mass of flesh upon the grass. Suddenly, without warning, another shot rang out and I thought this was indeed my last supper. I didn't feel much pain from what I thought was a bullet going into my body. As I looked up I saw the crazed gunman fall to the ground bleeding profusely from his chest. Surprised that it wasn't me who was shot, I felt a bit traumatized myself. In reality it was one of my bodyguards who came out from behind another tree on the side of my house that shot the crazed man. My bodyguards were supposed to be watching over me, but they were in the backyard at the time they heard the shot rang out and they rushed out just in time to save my life. One of the bodyguards, with his immense training and quick reaction, shot the deranged man in the chest. I was not shot, just sprawled out on the ground after my jump and my bullet wound was merely a small stick that went into my stomach when I landed on the grass.

I quickly shook myself off and went over to the man who was literally shaking from the bullet wound that went through his chest and it appeared to exit from his back. He was lying on his side convulsing in a heap of flesh and blood; the bodyguards and I were in astonishment over what we witnessed.

I instructed one of the bodyguards to take the demented man's gun and handcuff him. Defiantly the bodyguard squealed, "Why would I handcuff this man, can't you see his body is ripped to shreds?" he yelled.

I shouted back my instructions as calmly as I could without losing my cool and I warned him, "Quickly, do what I'm telling you now!" He hesitated and I screamed, "Did you hear me, do it quickly or he will die!" I said.

With a look of blatant seriousness he saw in my eyes, he obeyed. The bodyguard pulled the injured man's hands behind his back and handcuffed him. By this time the crazed gunman was quivering more violently. I pulled out my wallet, and with my hands trembling so bad I could almost not control myself, I somehow managed to get a wooden stick out. These special sticks are about the same size as a toothpick and extremely sharp on both ends. It was wrapped the same way as individual toothpicks are wrapped for restaurants. When I finally unwrapped the stick, I knelt down beside the bleeding man and told him, "You are not going to die, at least not today anyway!" And with that, I pierced the wooden stick directly into his shoulder area. As the stick sank deep into his pale skin, an instantaneous calmness came over his body and the violent shaking stopped. The bleeding stopped in the blink of an eye!

"Oh my God," shrieked one of the bodyguards. "How did you do that!"

"This is the reason you are protecting me," I answered back. I was amazed and astonished just as much as they were. Still, there was blood all over the clothes of the delusional man. Out of curiosity I ripped open the crazed man's shirt and, using the clean part of it, I wiped away the blood from his chest. "Nothing, nothing!" I blurted out. In utter amazement we looked on in incomprehension; there was absolutely no gunshot wound. The wound was completely gone, completely healed! It was as though nothing had happened to the crazed man's body. Wide-eyed, I looked at the man in great sorrow and relief at the same time and I asked him how he felt.

With a gurgle in his voice he kind of stammered and said, "I'm just shaken up, but I don't feel any pain at all." In amazement we all looked at each other in an out-of-sequence type of gaze. The whole ordeal only lasted a short time and yet it seemed the whole incident lasted a long time. I asked the bodyguard to sit him up comfortably and the other bodyguard commented it was a good idea about putting on the handcuffs in advance. I gave him a wink and heard the sirens come roaring down the street.

About six police cars stormed onto the scene. Quickly bailing out of their patrol cars, they came scurrying up to where we were all standing and they saw the crazed man lying on the ground, handcuffed, bloodied, and ready to be taken away. One of the police officers asked me if we needed to call for an ambulance and I told him it wouldn't be necessary. The officer then asked me if I thought the man would be able to stand and I said he was perfectly physically able, although he was probably shaken up. Two officers put on plastic gloves and they lifted him up and began to question us about what took place.

The first thing I said was, "You're not going to believe this but…"

Just then the handcuffed maniac crowed, "Believe him! Each and every word he says is true, I swear on my life! He must be some kind of a deity or miracle worker, but whatever he is all I can say is a few minutes ago I was lying on the ground with a bullet hole in my chest dying and now I'm completely healed."

The bodyguards looked like Casper the Friendly Ghost at the whole ordeal they had just witnessed and whispered to me, "We've got to talk!"

"We will," I replied.

One of the policemen questioned, "Hey, are you the man who's been on all the magazine covers and television shows?"

"Yes," I said humbly, "I am."

"Well that explains a lot of what has taken place here, doesn't it?" he said. With a gleam in his eye, I knew he was pretty well-versed on what had just transpired. For sure this was just another not-so-typical day in my life that I had been living. The next few hours were spent with me giving accounts of what had happened and then newspaper reporters showing up for a story.

"I know it's hard to believe," I told the reporters. "I myself was stunned over what took place! I know you have doubts and you're thinking the story I told you is impossible and you won't allow yourself to believe it even if you try with your entire mind. If you didn't see it for yourself you wouldn't believe it and I don't blame you because I wouldn't believe it either! I know I can't convince you or force you to believe what just took place, but maybe if you read my story of how all this began you will see that maybe miracles can come true. There is a rational reason for the phenomena that took place here today. This is one of those unknown doors that we can choose to open up and walk through or we can shut our eyes and never come to a point of belief. Fear, unbelief, doubt, all these come to mind, but only by walking down a path will we ever get to a mountaintop. This journey is an adventure that will blow your mind, rattle your fears, and turn your unbelief upside-down. You can cast your doubt into the wind if you will only let your mind have the opportunity to think things through reasonably. Let us embark on this fascinating journey, hand-in-hand and learn something new about ourselves," I explained to them.

I told the reporters that they needed to read my documents that were given to every major media network in the world to fully understand what I was talking about. I asked them to research it thoroughly so they would be able to accurately report what happened there that day. I told them where they could go to get the information that I had printed up firsthand. I pleaded with them to report on everything precisely as I felt people's lives were at stake in what they reported to the public. After all the information was given and the reporters left, I went back inside the house to clean myself up. I took a shower first and afterwards I kneeled beside my bed and gave thanks to the Lord for sparing my life that day. After praying to my Heavenly Father, I felt compelled to write my complete story from day one of what had taken place in my life. I knew it would take some time to write so everywhere I went I had my computer notebook with me.

This is the account of my fascinating story. My narrative really begins long ago, right after the death of Jesus Christ of Nazareth. A certain rich man at that time in history named Joseph, who himself believed in Jesus, came from the town of Arimathea and asked Pilate, who was the Governor of Judea at that time, for the body of Jesus Christ. After receiving permission from Pilate to take the body, Joseph took Jesus's body to his own tomb, which he had built especially for himself. The tomb was cut out of a rock and was magnificent for that day and age. Joseph then wrapped the Lord's body in a clean linen cloth and rolled a big huge stone over the entrance of the tomb. The stone, once in place, would be nearly impossible to move because of its size, weight and position.

Now Joseph was respected as a good and upright man in that town. He was looked upon as decent and kindhearted. The story of what Joseph did for the Lord has been told many times over and over again throughout history. Many Sunday school teachers all over the world have told children of how Joseph took great care in the burial of the Lord Jesus Christ. But another story, known to only a few at that time, still lingers on to this very day. The story is told that some believe that Joseph not only took the body of Jesus, but that he also took the wooden cross that Jesus was crucified on, along with Jesus's body. And according to this legend, Joseph cut the wooden cross into smaller pieces and then hid the cross deep into the mountains of Israel, where only he knew the whereabouts. Joseph went on to eternity without ever telling a soul where the cross was hidden.

My name is David Clayton and the part of my story begins when, as a wealthy young American businessman, I was touring Israel, a country that I dearly love. While visiting the Holy Land, I was told about this mysterious legend of long ago. I was so intrigued by the story that I promised myself I would come back to search for this great archeological find and reveal it to the world. Because of the cross's great significance to mankind and the history of the event that touched the lives of every human being on the planet from then, I promised myself that I would find this most important piece of historical wood. I will tell this story in my own words because the world longs to hear the accounts of what led up to become the most talked about and enthralling events to ever happen in our lifetime. Because I am not the greatest writer in the world and am just a businessman, please bear with me, as this is my personal account of what has transpired in my life.

# THE CROSS

My story started when I returned to America with great enthusiasm about trying to find the cross of Jesus Christ. I was eager to get an exploration team together and go back to Israel to be a part of the greatest archeological hunt in history and possibly of all time. Even though I was a very successful businessman, deep down in my heart I always longed to be an archeologist. As a child I loved digging in the dirt and looking for hidden treasures that I thought for sure were there somewhere. I was a great optimist as a young child; for example, I would ask my playmates while on the playground, "Would you like to find a ten dollar bill on the ground?" Of course they would say yes and then I would answer, "Not me, because if I didn't find a ten dollar bill on the ground here, then on my way home I would find a hundred dollar bill." It never made sense to the other kids, but to me I always felt that if I passed up on something and wasn't selfish about it, then something greater would come my way as a result of my selflessness.

But my dreams of digging for gold were never realized as my father left me the inheritance of his soft drink company. My father was a perfectionist and always thought he could do things better. So when he wanted to start his own cola distributing company, he named it Fresh Refreshment Company. His thinking was that any kind of drink you buy should be fresh and refreshing. When I was just a young boy I remember him laughing and saying, "The world wants a better cola and I'm going to give it to them even fresher and more refreshing than they could ever dream of." So with that name, his determination and hard work he set up to become the king of colas. Everything he touched turned to gold and so began another one of my father's business ventures.

My dad always wanted me to take over the family business some day, although he knew that deep down in my heart I loved archaeology and would rather have pursued that as a career. But because of my father's persistence, I agreed to get a college degree in Business Management. It may have worked out for the best because my father died when I was only 30 years old and that left me in complete control of all his businesses. Unlike my father though, I set up the businesses with skillful management so that they would be able to run themselves without me always having to be there for them to be successful. That way I could pursue other interests and still keep my word to my father by running the businesses.

My mother had recently been bed ridden by a stroke and was barely able to move because of paralysis. I hired a full-time live-in nurse to take care of her and I visited her whenever possible. I was always close to my mother so we spent a lot of time together during my adult life. Yet, I was feeling bored by the business life, and like a fish thrown out into the desert heat my brain was stagnating as a businessman. All I wanted was to be back in the ocean again swimming in schools of excitement, and the world of archaeology tugged at my heart strings. So I gathered an excellent team together of experts in the fields of history and archaeology and together we studied the maps of Israel. We used any and all means possible as we strived to find information about where Joseph of Arimathea hid the cross that Christ died on two thousand years ago.

For me personally this meant spending hours devouring the Bible. Although I have always believed what the Bible says and was raised in church, I never came to realize for myself totally that it was factual that Jesus truly did indeed rise from the dead. I enjoyed church and believed what I thought was right, but somehow it wasn't a really personal thing like some people spoke of. My family never realized that I was by all accounts just a churchgoer. I thought I knew a lot about the Bible as a child, but now after reading so much I realized I didn't know as much as I thought I did. Of course during this time of the archaeological hunt I came to learn many other things about God, but since my mission was to find the cross it made learning about Jesus's resurrection all the more astounding! I figured we would never find His body because it probably wasn't there anymore, because if the body of Jesus were ever found then that meant He didn't rise from the dead. And because the claims that Jesus rose from the dead were so controversial at that time in history I would think that his adversaries would have done everything in their power to find His body and prove the whole event as a hoax. Of course nobody did ever find His body, which goes to show there is some truth to the claims of His disciples. But somehow I strangely wondered why no one ever tried to find the cross? It was almost like a mission to me, a mission that was a life or death episode as far as I was concerned. Because of the prompting that I felt, I spared no expense to make sure it would be successful. I was so utterly determined to find the cross that it became my entire life.

# THE HOLY LAND

After months and months of intense study, my team and I headed off for Israel. We landed at a time when the weather was absolutely gorgeous. I had pre-prepared all the arraignments for the entire team. Because of this we were able to go right away to the place where we would be staying for our entire time there. The trip was exhausting for me mostly because I never did feel comfortable flying in an airplane. It just seems unnatural for a human being to be up in the air like as if we were birds or something. You know the old saying that if God intended for us to fly He would have given us wings. Well, I really felt that way. So while the others slept, I would sit there with eyes wide open, unable to sleep and I was exhausted. I even took two over-the-counter sleeping pills, which did absolutely nothing for me. After a few hours of not being able to sleep, I took two more sleeping pills and still sat there with my eyes wide open. I would have paid to get some sleep during that flight to Israel. My back ached and I longed to just lay flat instead of in a sitting position hour after hour. If I could have lain down in the aisle then maybe I could have fallen asleep. As a result of my sleeping battle on the plane, I slept soundly once we reached our destination.

The next morning I woke up inspired. I walked out into the sun just as it was beginning to rise and something felt like it was arising within my heart as well. The sun was bright, crisp and overpowering. My senses sprang to new life as I looked on what was the most beautiful sunrise I had ever beheld. There was something supernatural about this land and my spirit responded to its allure. I felt new and alive, the excitement welled up inside me as though I was just born and knew it. I took my time to let it all soak deep into my body; I was saturated into something that was larger than me. There was something here that was beyond what I could have ever imagined. There was a power that seemed to overtake me and all I could do was receive it. I seemed powerless in what I was experiencing and I didn't want what was happening to me to ever go away. I welcomed this supernatural power, which brought feelings I had never thought possible, into my being.

The team was ready to go now after we had a great breakfast. We met with our guides and left for the adventure I longed and hungered for. Our first exploration brought us to mountains and caves that were majestic. The scenery was grandiose in nature and my eyes never beheld such natural beauty. I had told myself that even if we didn't find the cross that Jesus was crucified on that this was the adventure that would bring me satisfaction and allow my restlessness to be brought to an end. Our first day out yielded no cross, but we were intrigued and fascinated by the things we saw. The beauty of nature was exhilarating. I felt like I was in my glory; my dreams of being an archeologist were being fulfilled. How I would love the life of doing this each and every day.

When the sun was beginning to set, I experienced what could only be known as something that was astonishing. I was in complete rapture over the overwhelming gorgeous sunset. Something was happening to me as I gazed steadily into the eyes of what felt like was my one true love and I fell into its spell like a baby being cuddled for the first time in the arms of a loving mother. My heart longed for the things I was feeling like a baby is comforted by the mother's heartbeat. It was almost as if a crater had opened up in my heart and it was being filled with what had been engulfing me since I arrived. My soul became the Grand Canyon and it was being filled with sunshine and warmth. I knew I was where I was supposed to be at this point in my life. We went back to our residences for the night and none of us were gloomy at all over the day we had. We knew it was a long shot and we recognized if we did find the cross it would be one of the most meaningful finds in archeological history.

After a few weeks of endless searching, we were still not deterred from our objective. The pure energy I felt from the beginning never declined and I was still beholden to its lure. I had to fly back to America to deal with some of Fresh Refreshment's business deals, while my team kept searching on. When I arrived back in the States, my mother wasn't getting any better. She seemed to be giving up and not gaining her strength back. I talked her into letting a physical therapist work with her to improve her moving ability and strength. Mother agreed she would get the help since I insisted. Back at my company it was work as usual, but my heart was still in Israel with my team of archeologists. By now they had been there for over three months and searched areas that were exceptionally hard to reach. They had even hired an older man who said he was from the Twelve Tribes of Israel and had some knowledge of where we should be looking. This gave me some hope that they would make some kind of a discovery soon.

When my business dealings were done, I caught the first flight back to Israel that I could find. When the plane landed I felt that same sensation as I had felt before. Like a kind of fulfillment and a peace that made me sense like I was in a deep sound sleep on a bed made of soft comfy feathers. I knew in my heart there was something here for me. I knew there was some kind of destiny for my life and this work I was doing was what was going to bring about my destiny. I loved this land and the rich history it held. It was captivating for me to be walking on the same soil as the Prophets of old walked. At times I felt I had to pinch myself that I was actually in Israel, the holy land of

Abraham, Isaac and Jacob. I wondered how anyone could defile this land and act like it was acceptable with them. This land seemed holy to me as my heart fell in love with the country and the people of Israel. I knew this land was the apple of God's eye and you could tell by the spirit that dwells upon the nation. Defilers feel no spirit and that is to their demise, but I was in love with this country and I couldn't get enough of it.

As the weeks passed by, I found myself being humbled to the point of kneeling down in prayer. I was raised in church, but this was something more than just going to church. I read a verse in Romans that said, "The creation waits in eager expectation for the sons of God to be revealed" (Romans 8:19). *Am I one of the sons of God that the creation is waiting on?* I wondered. It was my heart being molded like a piece of pottery spinning round and round just giving in to the majestic anointing and I read the Bible almost constantly. I also read in Romans, "Does not the potter have the right to make out of the same lump of clay some pottery for noble purposes and some for common use?" (Romans 9:21). I marveled, *Is God going to make me a common piece of pottery or a piece for noble purposes?* I questioned. Who are we as human beings that we are allowed the privilege to either accept or reject God? God permits us this privilege and even if we reject Him, He doesn't respond by taking our life. He is patient, kind and loving to the human race. It is His desire that one day we would all change our minds and come to Him with humbleness in our hearts. Something seemed different now within me and this time it was not because I was trying to find the cross of Jesus Christ, but rather I was trying to find the Jesus Christ who died on the cross. I was not trying to find an object, but I was trying to find Jesus, who was the object of my faith!

## MY PERSONAL SEARCH

This power I was feeling actually was leading me to places where we had searched before for the cross and now I was returning to look again. Somehow that seemed appropriate in light of the fact that

that's exactly what was going on in within my heart. It was kind of like the children's game where one child looks for something and the other child tells him if he is getting hotter or colder in the hunt. It made me realize that during my childhood I had made somewhat of an attempt to search for truth as a churchgoer, but now I was in the process of returning and searching again. I remembered a poem I wrote as a younger man that said: "Whenever I hurt, whenever I sorrow, I'll always stay close and dream about tomorrow." This was a poem about God and staying close to Him, but now it was becoming a reality in my life. I was hungering for more of God and my search for the material cross was just as fervent as my search for the invisible cross that each of us needs to find within our hearts.

This Jesus who died on the cross I was trying to find was actually striving to find me. I was on a pursuit for the cross and Jesus was pursuing me! That reality was like childhood dreams where you are able to fly and the exhilaration of floating in the air is incredible. Knowing that God would take the time to seek me out was awe inspiring. I opened my heart to allow Him to find me and a miraculous event happened, "For this son of mine was dead and is alive again; he was lost and is found" (Luke 15: 24). I thought I was looking for the historical Jesus who died on the cross and in my search I found the forever-living Jesus who still lives today. I began to understand the feelings I had of emptiness before. My search for the cross went on, but my search for peace and fulfillment ended. I found it!

I prayed one evening that my heart would be like a garden, with the word of God as the seed planted within my garden and the Holy Spirit would be the rain that makes the seeds grow. My heart bloomed like a flower in the desert. Here in Israel, who could have ever thought this could happen to me. I had made all these plans for my life and yet here I was with a totally new mindset and new direction for my life. My heart yearned for knowledge of God; my pride died when I met the Creator of the Universe. I asked God to help me in my search for the cross, but whatever the outcome would be I would always love God for this rebirth within my soul.

After a few more days of exhausting searches I felt kind of disheartened because we had not had any success. My spiritual life had become a great success, but our physical search for the cross was starting to wear on us. That evening we went to our residences, and I prayed before going to bed like I usually do, but this time with more fervency. I felt weary and I told God that maybe I was wrong to be doing this. Possibly if I found the cross people would worship it instead of God? Maybe this was all for my own triumph, for my pride and not because I truly wanted to bring glory to God? An impression deep within me whispered for me not to give up and I was strengthened as I prayed.

I went into a deep sound sleep that was so peaceful even a fright train rumbling down worn-out tracks with a stuck whistle could not have woken me up. I had a dream that I was looking for buried treasure; I found a treasure chest buried on a piece of land, but I could not take it off the land or others would see it. I covered the treasure back up with dirt and sold everything I had to buy this land. People thought I was crazy to buy a worthless piece of land that had no value, especially since I had to sell all my belongings to purchase it. After the deed was mine I uncovered my new treasure with great delight. The price I paid for the land was not even close to the rewards I found buried in that treasure. I sold everything and gained everything! I woke up from that dream with an outlook of hope and peace.

## BURIED TREASURE

That morning the team and I left to go to our next excavation site. The older man from the Twelve Tribes of Israel said he wanted us to go to a place where no one would ever look because the land was not too mountainous with caves. When we arrived I questioned his decision to look in the area, because there was no place to hide anything there. "Just give it a few hours," he said. With that our search began. I wondered over to a place that looked like a dirt path. It looked like a road that someone had raked out. I followed the path for about a quarter mile and then found an intersecting dirt path that didn't lead to anywhere in particular. How strange this looked to me and I suddenly felt like a child playing the game of hotter and colder. Like I was getting closer yet unable to find anything. An incredible panic came over me and I felt sick and nauseated. I started to vomit profusely and I thought the sun had gotten to me. On my knees hacking and coughing I tried to get up the strength to walk. But I could not stand up, I wasn't able to walk!

I yelled out for help but the others were too far away to hear me. I looked up at the sun, whose bright crisp rays penetrated through me like a huge magnifying glass hovering above me. My eyesight started to go dim and all I could see were shadows. Here I was all by myself sick, not able to stand and almost blind. I knew how the Apostle Paul felt when he was blinded on the Damascus road. *Maybe this is the Damascus road*, I thought. *Maybe an angel will come to me and heal me with some kind of miraculous spiritual experience.* Paul was blinded but he was eventually healed by the prayer of a righteous man who was sent by God. Nothing happened to me though as I slouched there in the sun wondering what was going on.

Whenever I'm in trouble I pray, and so I prayed to the Lord to bring me help. I wish I could say suddenly I jumped up completely healed, or that I had some angel visit me and lift up on my feet, but it didn't happen that way. I started crawling, nauseated and hardly able to see where I was going. The heat was pounding down on me like a pro wrestler going down for the last time. I felt like I was burning up inside, like flames had engulfed my entire being. Weak and unable to go any further, I passed out flat on my back sprawled out on the dirt. I thought about how the man in the New Testament felt when he was robbed and beaten. They left him for dead lying on a road by himself. It was by the love of the Good Samaritan who saw him and had compassion on him that saved his life. I hoped that my team of Good Samaritans would find me soon.

The group had been going in the opposite direction as I was headed, and after they didn't see me for a long time, they started to wonder where I was. They decided to turn around to find me and so they walked and walked to where they found me passed out, flat on my back in the dirt. They washed my face off with water and gave me something to drink. Slowly my sight started to come back to normal as I explained to them what happened. I ate a piece of fruit to give me strength and then tried to see if I could stand up. My knees were very weak, but I managed with help to stand. We started to head back to our vehicles when I turned around to look back at where I had gotten sick. The strangest feeling came over me when I saw in the two dirt roads intersecting together, because it looked like a big cross in the dirt. I shouted to the others to look at the intersecting roads and they all said, "So what!"

"So what!" I responded. "Doesn't it look like a big cross to you?" One of the men pointed out that I was delusional because of being sick and he said I was suffering from a heatstroke. I told them I wanted to go back to that area and look around some more. With some convincing we did and there was nothing anywhere to be found. I told them to start digging in the middle of where the two roads met. The men took turns digging and they dug for a few hours with nothing found. We decided to stop for the day because we were exhausted and didn't find anything so we headed back home. We ate a nice dinner and I wanted to get back to my room just to lie down on a soft mattress. It didn't take long until I was fast asleep. I dreamed that I was walking down a path and fell into some kind of pit. The hole seemed to come out of nowhere and swallow me up. I started to holler for help, but as I howled I startled myself awake. Wondering what the meaning of the dream was, I decided that we had to return to the same place where we started digging that day.

The next morning we returned to the hole and kept digging it deeper. It was tiresome and after many hours of just digging a deep hole we were about to give up. The men were grumbling because the dirt was too hard to dig by hand. I decided that we needed to get some kind of backhoe equipment if we were to have any success at all. We stopped early for the day to get the equipment needed for the next day. The following morning we started earlier than usual and dug a deeper and wider hole with the backhoe. Still, after hours of nothing we all agreed to fill the hole back up with dirt when just as we were about to start filling it in one of the men with a shovel down inside the hole poked his shovel in the dirt and soil started flowing into what seemed like a hollow cave below. The man cried out, "I found something!" We kept digging a larger hole big enough to climb into.

As we cleared the dirt out of the cave-like crevice, there were a few stairs carved out from the dirt that led down only a few feet. The cave was so small at this point that only one of the men could go in at a time. He had to hand dig and pass buckets of dirt up through the opening to us to empty them out. The archeologist screamed with great excitement that he found something. On the bottom of the cave was a wooden box wrapped with some kind of covering to keep the box preserved. We had to dig more of the top of the small cave out to try to lift the box. This took hours because as he dug, we had to haul up the dirt bucket by bucket. When the cave seemed big enough, we tied ropes around the box and pulled it up the steps, slow and steady. When the box reached the section near the top of the steps, we were all filled with adrenaline and pulled the box out as if our life depended on it. When we had it on the ground, we were all screaming with excitement and jubilation. Jumping up and down around the box, we were like children who had just won their first championship baseball game.

All of the sudden the ground started to implode over the cave. We pulled the box away from the area and watched in amazement at what was happening. It was like a mini earthquake right there in front of us. The whole ground didn't shake, it just shook over the cave alone. It seemed to sink into the ground looking like one of those sand timers. We moved away from the vicinity because it seemed to be holy ground. It appeared as though God was covering up the cave by His own power and might. It just imploded, and when it was completely covered there was no more commotion just a silence that made all of us realize we had just witnessed the mighty hand of God.

After this happened we were all in elation at the sight we had just beheld. I instructed the men to finish covering the spot so no one could tell where we were digging. After finishing, we carried the wooden box back to our vehicles and loaded it on one of the trucks and headed back to our house.

The trip back to our quarters was filled with great anticipation. We were like a bunch of high school cheerleaders, high-fiving each other with big grins notably stuck on our faces. My heart was racing madly at what could be in the box. When we arrived home, I instructed one of the team to videotape the opening of the box and another to photograph each scene. We set up special lighting so that nothing would interfere with the quality of what was going to be revealed. The expert archeologists then took over operations with extreme care. They dusted off the outside of the box and found an inscription on the outside. Hurriedly, we called for our Elder Jewish expert to read us the inscription. His interpretation flooded my heart like a valentine being given to me by the most beautiful girl in my fourth grade class. He read it with a heavy Jewish accent that made it all the more meaningful, he read: "The Cross of Jesus of Nazareth, born in Bethlehem in Judea."

My eyes welled up with tears over what I just heard. Partly because the fact that it said where Jesus was born and partly because of knowing that He was crucified. I remembered a poem I wrote after realizing the great love God has for us. It went like this: "Jesus stole my heart one day with all the things he said. Then he gave it back to me with joy and peace instead. He lives their still today after all this time. Jesus stole my heart one day and I gave it back to him."

By this time I was overwhelmed with great joy about what was happening. With extreme carefulness, we opened the box slowly, documenting each step we took. The first cover we took off the box revealed another box inside. This box too was covered in with some kind of special wrapper to preserve it. We carefully opened the cover of the box and found yet another box inside with another special covering to preserve it as well. All these preservatives were then placed in specially sealed archeological boxes we brought for preservation. I thought it was somehow fitting that if it was the cross inside, it was packaged in three boxes. Kind of like it was a meaning that was relative to when Jesus was in the grave for three days before He rose from the dead.

We opened the next box and inside was cut up pieces of wood. From my archeological studies, I knew this is what the cross would have looked like, except it was cut down into smaller pieces. The team and I laid out the wood in the shape it fitted to and it was definitely a cross that was used for a crucifixion. Whether it was the cross of Jesus Christ we could not be sure, in spite of the inscription on the outside of the box. However, we all knew that whoever buried this went to great lengths to keep it hidden and well-preserved. We took hundreds of pictures and small samples that were loose off the cross for studies. When the cross was laid out in its rightful shape, we could see that on both the right hand and left hand area were nail holes, the foot area also had a nail hole in it. Strangely there were no nails in the box and so we assumed that during that time they reused the nails for other crucifixions.

## BACK TO AMERICA

The next few days were spent in taking special care to place the cross pieces in highly specialized boxes made to keep such findings intact. My legal representative made sure we would not have any problem in leaving the country with our discovery. When we had everything ready to go, I hired our own passenger plane back to the United States to insure that the cross would be with me and would not get lost or stolen.

I had prepared the team and hand picked the group of men whom I could trust to keep silent about the discovery. Long before the expedition started, I explained to them how we would handle the cross and what I required of them during and after our venture. They were well-prepared to follow the instructions laid out. Bonuses were given to all the team and the amount spent so far was well over a million dollars. I also gave future bonuses in time sequences to ensure that all the team members held total silence. The time had come to head back to America and we had around eight men put the boxes into the plane for our long flight back. The plane flight home seemed an eternity to me as I was in great anticipation to find out if the cross was authentic and to see if the dating of it coincided with the time of the death of Jesus Christ.

When we landed at the airport I had my secretary arrange for a truck to load up the crates, and my limousine picked us up and whisked us off to the lab I leased out for this remarkable find. Preparations were made already for the scientists to test the cross and try to preserve it to the best of their ability. The lab was inside a guarded gate that looked like a military wing for special investigations and that's why I chose it. My hand-picked scientists were experts in the field of dating archeological pieces. Everything was videotaped for proof of the process used, to please the skeptics in the future. My instructions were to spare no expense at the testing and examining of this great historical piece of wood. The testing would last a few weeks before we would know for sure if the cross was authentic.

During the wait I had my lawyers get ready for any lawsuits anyone would try, especially Israel. I had taken all the legal requirements required by their country by getting the proper permits to do archeological diggings there and hired a certain local company in Israel that helped us make the discovery. I made sure that all my tracks were covered in case we found the cross and I did so with utter respect to all laws within both countries, Israel and the United States. I made painstaking efforts to insure that we did not disturb anything that would upset the countrymen of Israel. I went through anguishing days during that time over these legal issues. I had never felt so much pressure not only for my responsibility to the people, but my responsibility to God also. I was a perfectionist and if it took years to do this correctly I would have done so.

The next few nights were terrible for me, I sweated, I tossed and turned; I was a mess thinking about what we could have found. I prayed for mercy from God to protect me from harm in case I disturbed something He didn't want disturbed. Kind of like the movie about finding the Ark of the Covenant. I didn't want anything to happen in my life because I disturbed a holy site. I told God I would be willing to do whatever He wanted me to do with the cross. I completely forgot about Fresh Refreshment Company because I was so wrapped up in the all the happenings.

I visited the lab daily, which had become like a militarized zone. No one was allowed in without being checked and no one was allowed out without being checked. It was so strict sometimes even I couldn't get in without proper identification. Finally, the results started to come in and I wasn't sure if I was mentally prepared to know the answer or not.

Our group went into a meeting room to look at the test results and I felt like I was hyperventilating. I was so nervous my hands were trembling. The head archeologist took control of the meeting and he said it was determined that the cross was dated for around the same time historically that Jesus of Nazareth died on a wooden cross in the land of Israel two thousand years ago. However, he cautioned, no one could say 100 percent that it was beyond doubt the cross of Jesus Christ.

My body was in overdrive at this point and jittery. It was as though I drank a few pots of coffee. I addressed the team with the plan of action that was ahead. It was time to make this revelation; it was time to make this finding known to everyone in the world. No one lights a lamp on a hill and covers it, but uses it for light. Jesus said in Luke 8:16: "No one lights a lamp and hides it in a jar or puts it under a bed. Instead, he puts it on a stand so that those who come in can see the light." This miracle was going to be used by God for His glory and honor unto Himself. Little did I know at this time that it would bring for me a new world of insane madness along with the joy that it would bring.

I had my company lawyers make ready the unveiling of the most wonderful, glorious discovery the world had ever seen. They prepared the day of the unveiling with great responsibility, like the priests did for the Ark of the Covenant. Television stations from around the globe and reporters would be covering this historical phenomenon. The night before the world was to see the actual cross of what many of us on the team believed to be the real cross of Jesus Christ seemed endless. I was in earnest prayer over what God had given me and for the first time in awhile I heard a still small voice inside me telling me to be at peace for this was all in God's plan. I was weak at the time I was spoken to, whether it was in my mind or verbally I don't know. All I know is what was said to me, and I had a supernatural peace that beats all understanding.

I answered back to God in a little song I made up, "Heavenly Father, I pray for a song, one about joy and a love come true. One of peaceful dreams of living with you." I slept that night in a violently peaceful way. Violence and peace are the only way for me to describe how deep and sound my rest was. Like a bear hibernating for the winter, God was preparing me for the storms ahead. I woke up the next morning like a hungry bear that would do anything for food. My appetite was wet and my hunger mean. I was a man on a mission compelled with great strength from on high to do what I was called to do. I stretched out my heart to God and He answered me back with His blessings. My life had just begun and I really didn't know how much it would change.

# CHAPTER 2
# The Cross Revealed

Today was the day of the great unveiling. The event was to be broadcasted throughout the entire nation. The news interviewer was a well-known news personality famous in America. I asked him to be nice to me during questioning. I didn't want to be put on the spot with questions that were not relevant to what was going to be shown to the world. Tracy, my business assistant, was by my side as she usually is. She has always been with me during situations that I may need her help. I was introduced first and the interview went pretty good. I explained how we had found the cross and the scientists on hand explained their testing procedures. The broadcast was live from the lab and the location was not disclosed for safety and security reasons. It was the most-watched television show in the history of America for that time.

The show created such a stir that I became the most wanted man for interviews. In a matter of days I went on to become the most talked about personality worldwide. Talk shows argued about whether it was really the cross of Jesus or not. Problems came about for certain religions that did not want the cross of Jesus to be a proven fact. People who didn't believe in God were horrified over the thought of what this could mean for them. The broadcast spread quickly around the entire world and other countries began to get caught up in the cyclone. Major religions that had denounced that Jesus was crucified were up in arms over the discovery. It created such a commotion that the entire world was reeling from the news like a drunkard stumbling down the street. Arguments were breaking out over the issue of the cross and people were quarreling about it constantly.

Newspapers clamored for more insights about what should be done with the cross. It was the biggest news event in history and I was a wanted man. I, David Clayton, became the most sought after man in the entire world. I had become a religious icon in one day.

I was getting death threats and had to hire professional bodyguards to protect me. I was being worshipped by people as some kind of a new Messiah. Out of what I thought would help the world, came a world for myself that was so intense that it was hard to be me anymore. I thought I had this whole thing planned out pretty good, but I never thought it would cause such a stir as it did. I had advisers that met with me over what should be done with the cross. We decided that the public wanted to see it so bad that we would have it enclosed in protective glass and bring it to each state in the country. All viewers would have to pay a minimal fee to see it and the money would be split with the churches in each state it went to and with Israel because we were indebted to Israel for all their help. We quickly put together a plan for the "Tour of the Cross." Soon it was up and running within a short amount of time.

The cross made its appearance to the States and was protected like it was a nuclear bomb. I showed up every once in awhile to do interviews in certain cities. People would ask me to pray for them; they thought I was some kind of saint. I had people grab at my clothes and rip pieces from my shirt. Even my hairstylist, whom I call Di for short, auctioned off my hair on the internet. I'm not sure how much she got, but for her sake I hoped it was a lot because she was my long-time stylist and a good friend of mine. Some people screamed praise to me while others yelled out obscenities. I had to really humble myself before God during this time. The pressure was incredible, but God gave me His grace to get through it.

It took a few months for the cross to make its way through America. While it was in Washington D.C., I was invited to the White House to meet the President of the United States. He was a great man who believed in the Bible himself. That was an experience I shall never forget. I was given awards, plaques, streets named after me and keys to some cities. I didn't seek this kind of attention, but it sought me. I guess God had His plan for what was going on and what would come; all I could do was try to live humbly before Him.

# HEALING STICK

I needed a few days away from all the commotion, so I went to see my mom and visit for a few days. I figured that a rest away from the excitement would do me good. I stayed at my mother's house while she was in a care center. My second day home I called my sister and asked her if she wanted to come over for dinner, but she said she had been very sick with the flu so she couldn't come over. That evening alone in my mother's house, I was cooking my own supper. Tracy asked me if I wanted to go out to eat, but I didn't want to deal with being seen. I decided to make a gourmet meal with fresh vegetables. I always enjoyed listening to quiet music while doing things around the house. It felt great to just be back home and not have all the commotion that I had been having lately.

As I was cutting up some vegetables, I cut my thumb open with a very sharp knife. Blood came gurgling out; quickly I grabbed a kitchen cloth and wrapped it around my hand. I looked in my mother's bathroom cabinets for band-aids but I couldn't find any. I put some hydrogen peroxide on the cut and it about made me jump through the roof. I left the towel wrapped around my thumb for a while to stop the bleeding. Usually I carry a band-aid in my wallet just in case I need one. As I was fumbling through my wallet looking for a band-aid I stuck myself in the finger with a splinter of wood, which I had taken off the cross because there were some loose pieces on it about the size of toothpicks. I thought they were unique so I pulled the sticks off and put them in my wallet. One of the wooden sticks jabbed into my finger, so when I pulled my finger out of the wallet, the stick was still hanging from my finger like a splinter. I felt an unusual sensation go through my body like electricity flooding my being. Instantly I took off the towel around my hand and the bleeding from my thumb stopped. I wiped the blood off under the sink faucet and there was no gash in my thumb.

I almost fainted at the sight of what had just taken place. I was flabbergasted and in utter amazement. The feeling was kind of eerie and I didn't comprehend what just took place. I always had one of my nostrils clogged up at all times and it was no longer clogged. I was breathing normal for the first time in as long as I could remember. I looked down below my knee where I'd had a bruise for a few days and it was gone. I have always had great constant pain in my lower back and it was gone. Somehow I was instantly healed when the stick from the cross stuck into my skin. I burst out in a chorus of praise shouting, "It was a healing stick!" My mind raced over many different thoughts of what really happened. *One minute I had a deep cut and was bleeding all over the place and the next minute there was no cut! I still had blood from the cut on me but when I wiped it off there was no cut and no more blood coming out.* I rehearsed this in my brain trying to figure it all out.

This was incredibly astonishing and I didn't know how to take it. I dropped to my knees thanking and worshipping God for what He did to me. This was just too amazing for my comprehension; overwhelmed I spent the next hour on my knees in the bathroom praising God for being so wonderful and kind to me. I didn't really know if it was just God doing some kind of miracle or if it was the stick from the cross that healed me. When I finally got up from my knees I felt hungry and so I finished cooking dinner and spent the rest of the night reading my Bible.

The next morning I went to see my mother in the care center. I wanted to try a stick on her, but I knew if I brought it up to her she would think I was crazy. My mother was getting worse after her stroke and wasn't even able to walk. One side of her face was partially paralyzed as a result and it was hard for her to even talk. She slurred her words in discomfort, but she handled it well and always had a positive attitude over the whole ordeal. I told my mom what happened to me and asked her to put a stick in her mouth to see if it would heal her. She said okay, but she was kind of leery over the whole idea. After about ten minutes nothing happened and I was dumbfounded.

"I don't understand, Mother, why it didn't heal you. I'm going to go out to my car to get another stick, and I'll be back in a few minutes," I said. As I was walking out the door I heard my mother cry, "Ouch!"

"Son," she called, "I just stuck myself with your toothpick in my gums."

I turned to go back and noticed that on the side of her face where she was paralyzed was normal again. She said she felt completely better, even good enough to get out of bed.

"Mother," I asked, "how different do you feel?"

"Great," she responded, "I'm going to try to walk."

"Okay, Mother, let's try, but take it easy," I cautioned.

She sat up near the edge of the bed and stood up with no problem at all, and then she began walking.

"David," she shouted, "what on earth did you do to me?"

"I don't really understand it myself, Mother, but like I told you my cut last night was healed too. Do you remember how I could never breathe through both nostrils at the same time, well after I was poked by the stick I could breathe normal again!"

"Oh my God," she shouted. "David, look at my legs! All the bedsores I had on them are gone!"

"Mom, I'm so delighted for you, last night I had a bruise below my knee too and it was gone."

We hugged and Mom burst into tears crying. She said, "Look at me, David, I'm walking again. I can walk with no problems," she exclaimed. She was weeping out of sheer happiness. "David, why has God blessed us so? I don't feel any more pain in my body, it is a miracle for me to be standing without pain." We hugged each other again and cried together, and I told her I thought she would be able to go back to home.

"Mother, I need for you not to tell anybody what has happened to you. Just tell the center that you have been feeling better lately and you are ready to go home, okay? I have to have time to think about what happened to us, so it is very important that nobody knows," I told her. She gave me her promise and I checked her out of the center and we went home together.

That night was spent with great praise for God and what he had done for us. Both of us felt like we were in some kind of inspired state; it was like watching one of those movies where miraculous things happen and you sit there watching in utter amazement. We went to bed late that night and the next day I had a busy day ahead to try to figure out exactly what happened. Before I left my mother's house, I made sure she would be watched over and that she would tell nobody about our "little miracle."

## OH YE OF LITTLE FAITH

I went to one of my labs and immediately called my sister. I asked her to drive over to the lab, but she said she was too sick and when I explained to her about the healings, suddenly she was willing and agreed to take the drive. When Christa arrived I told her about how mom put a stick in her mouth and nothing happened. Then when she stuck herself with it she was instantly healed. "So I think that the healing came by penetrating into the skin," I explained. "I called you because I knew you were very sick and I wanted to experiment on you."

"Okay," she said, "I'll be your guinea pig, but I hope it doesn't hurt."

"Just sit down and we'll see what happens," I replied. I took out a stick and asked her to close her eyes and I quickly poked it in her arm.

"Ouch!" she screamed.

But nothing happened. I was shocked. "I don't understand it," I stuttered. "Maybe you don't have enough faith, Sis."

"Oh no, don't go blaming me for lack of faith. You know I believe in miracles even more than you do," Christa responded.

"Okay," I yielded, "I'll give you that, but what is going on?" I thought I had this thing figured out already. Christa went to lie down on the couch because she wasn't feeling so good. I rehearsed the healings over and over again in my mind, and I couldn't figure out what in the world was going on. *Let's see,* I contemplated to myself, *after I cut my thumb I went into the bathroom and pulled a band-aid out of my wallet and stuck myself with a stick, then later I cleaned up the blood around the sink and cleaned the stick and put it back into a lunch baggie. Then I went to see Mother at the care center and pulled another stick out of my wallet and gave it to her and she was healed.*

Suddenly it hit me like a parachutist jumping from a plane without a parachute. "Oh my word," I proclaimed loudly, "Christa, I stuck you with the same stick I stuck myself with!"

"So what, what does that mean?" she said. "It didn't work, did it?"

"Don't you see, the healing sticks can only heal once!" I reported.

"Are you sure you aren't just saying that so you can stick me again to pay me back for our childhood?" Christa retorted.

"No, Sis, no I'm not! I just wasn't thinking that maybe they only worked once, don't you see the significance?" I instructed.

"No," she responded, "I don't know what you're talking about."

"Remember that Jesus died on the cross, once for all time. He will never die again for the sins of mankind and so the wood from the cross only heals once! Keep in mind that Jesus cried out from the cross that fateful day: 'It is finished!' In other words, when God does something He does it once and for all."

"Hallelujah," she snapped, "let's try it again with a new stick!"

"Okay, Christa, drag yourself back over here and let's just see what happens."

"Maybe you should strap me in this time like a convicted killer being electrocuted for her punishment," she said sarcastically.

"No sarcasm, Sis, this is important. Close your eyes." One, two, three, and stab! Instantaneously Christa was healed of her fever.

"Oh my Lord," she shouted. "What just happened to me! I don't feel any fever whatsoever, it's totally gone." We sat amazed and stunned at the sight of her sitting there with no runny nose, no watery eyes, and no pink face.

I asked her, "Christa, do you have anything else physically ever wrong with you and if it so is it healed too?"

She responded, "Don't you remember I've had an extremely large and painful bunion on my left foot for many years? Let me take off my shoe and see if it's still there. David!" she screamed with the delight as a child going to Disneyland for the first time. "It's gone, it's gone, what in the world happened to me, oh my God I feel so new and painless. Maybe we could give one to Justin?" she proclaimed.

"Justin, now that would be the mother of all tests, wouldn't it?" I clamored.

"Think of it, if it healed his cancer that would be totally marvelous," Christa said.

"Wow, this is incredible, we have to be very quiet about this you know, because the cross is still on tour and if the public knew about this there would be mass hysteria," I said.

"David, did you see any blood on the cross when you found it?" Christa asked.

"No, I think it must have soaked into the wood and dried off I guess," I replied.

"Well, remember that the Bible says there is healing in the blood of Jesus," Christa said. "He was whipped with thirty-nine lashes on the back and I think there are thirty-nine different categories of diseases in the world today. The Bible says by His wounds we are healed (1 Peter 2:24)."

"So you think that when Jesus's blood flowed into the wood of the cross it saturated the wood with the healing power of God? Is that what you're trying to say?" I retorted.

"Yes, that's exactly what I mean," Christa answered excitedly.

"Kind of like when Paul the Apostle in the book of Acts touched handkerchiefs and aprons and gave them to the people they were healed. That is so incredible," I acknowledged. "We could have some kind of supernatural phenomena on our hands here. We have got to make a pact like I did with Mother to not tell anyone about this or else I'm afraid the cross will be ransacked by a flood of people. Do you understand what I am saying? This information would create a mass panic around the world for a piece of the cross. It's funny you know, the Bible says: 'The message of the cross is foolishness to those who are perishing, but to us who are being saved it is the power of God' (1 Corinthians 1:18). People think all this Jesus stuff is foolishness, but if they found out that the cross could heal them the same ones who don't believe would be the first ones to fight and kill over a piece of the cross, doesn't that strike you as peculiar?" I taught.

"You're right, David. I think you should try to get the cross back in your custody as soon as possible," Christa said.

"It's almost the end of the tour now anyways," I responded, "so I'll let the tour finish so it will not raise any suspicions. I've got a lot of planning to do and some more experiments, this raises a whole new issue of what should be done with the cross. Christa, do you think it should it be saved for its historical value or should it be cut up and used to heal the sick people of the world?" I questioned. "This is a huge responsibility and I have to ask for God's wisdom on what to do."

"I'm not sure, but it does my heart good to hear you say that," Christa answered. "I remember the time when you would have scoffed at all this Jesus stuff."

"That was before I started seeking truth in Israel, somehow a force bigger than myself influenced me and the Spirit of God seemed so loving and natural for me I responded. God seemed to teach me in a supernatural way while I was there and I matured very quickly. God is not weird in any sense, but rather He is normal and what He says for us in the Bible makes perfect sense for our lives. After I came to a point where I was down on my knees giving my life back to God I suddenly started to understand what it was He did for us on the cross. He sacrificed His life so we could live. He took the sins of the human race upon Himself so we could have forgiveness. Once I understood what a tremendous thing He had done for us, I started to fall in love with God instead of running from Him. I think the problem with many people is that God made it so simple for us that it is over our heads. We want to have to earn something; we never believe that anything could be given to us just because of love. It is difficult for us to receive freely God's grace just by merely asking by faith. Our hearts harden until something happens in our lives such as tragedy or suffering and then we decide that maybe God does love us, that is usually the starting point for Him to save us. Many people wonder why in the world does God have to send us a Savior, somebody to take away our sins. Why does God need some kind of sacrifice anyways they ask? Why can't He just accept us as the fragile human beings we are?"

"I've had a lot of people ask me that and I wasn't sure how to tell them in words they could understand," Christa responded.

"The reason why that is, is because when Adam and Eve first turned their backs on God and sinned in the Garden of Eden. God told Adam that, 'You are free to eat from any tree in the garden; but you must not eat from the tree of the knowledge of good and evil, for when you eat of it you will surely die' (Genesis 2:16-17). When Eve offered this delicious fruit to Adam, they both ate and they were suddenly both aware of their nakedness. But God said they would surely die and yet after they ate they were still physically alive. What really happened was they died spiritually that day; in other words the life of God that was within them had to depart because of their sin. Since God cannot dwell in sin His life left them and they died a spiritual death that day. They suddenly realized they were both naked, and so to cloth them, God had to kill an animal to make them clothes or coverings as the Bible says. Sure God could have made them clothes out of tree leaves if He wanted. But because of their sin something had to die and it was an innocent animal. God wanted Adam and Eve to see that as a result of their sin, death had to happen and so they were able to see the consequences of their sin. God shed the blood of animals and made garments of skin to clothe them. All because of their disobedience to the Lord God Almighty.

"Christa, remember that in The Old Testament it says, 'When God created man, he made him in the likeness of God?' (Genesis 5:1). Then later after the fall of man the Bible says, 'When Adam had lived 130 years, he had a son in his own image; and named him Seth' (Genesis 5:3). Notice that now instead of people being referred to as made in God's image, man was in the image of Adam. You can see that is because the Spirit and life of God is no longer dwelling in mankind, which is why the human race is born into a sinful nature. Then in the Old Testament they had to sacrifice an animal for the forgiveness of their sins once a year. This was a picture of what was to come. When Jesus came down to earth He had to be born of a virgin so that He would be born spiritually alive. Otherwise, if He was not born of a virgin He would have been born spiritually dead in the likeness of Adam just like all of us are. In the Bible it clarifies this by saying, 'the first man was from the dust of the earth (Adam), the second man from heaven (Jesus)' (1 Corinthians 15:47). 'The entire human race had to have their sin taken away and the Spirit of God restored within us, something had to die as a sacrifice in order to save us (kind of like clothing Adam and Eve) so we could have God's life in us again as Adam had in the beginning. That's why the New Testament proclaims, 'Consequently, just as the result of one trespass (Adam's sin) was condemnation for all men, so also the result of one act of righteousness (Jesus the Sacrificed Lamb) was justification that brings life for all men' (Romans 5:18). And again the Bible loudly declares, 'We know that we have been passed from death to life' (1 John 3:14)."

"I think if the average person could understand this then they would see how much love God has for them and they would respond," Christa replied.

"I guess the best way to explain it is how I always tell people who are struggling with the issue of why doesn't God just accept us in His kingdom; why did Jesus have to die for us? Well, to explain it as simple as I can, let me tell you a story that I don't remember if I heard it somewhere or I made it up myself. Let's say that you bought a brand-new house and paid thousands of dollars for the best, brightest white carpet on the market. You were very proud of the quality of the carpet and padding. Then I came knocking on your door to see your new house and it was raining outside. Now, my shoes were covered with mud from the rain and so when you opened the door you said to me, take your shoes off and come inside. Then I replied, why do I have to take my shoes off? Your response was that you had brand-new white carpeting and you didn't want it ruined. Then I said, well if you love me as your brother you should let me in regardless of whether or not my shoes are muddy. Then you said, it has nothing to do with you being my brother, all I want is for you to come in, but not for you to ruin my carpet. Still I hesitated. Then you even told me that you would be willing to untie my shoes for me and then put them on again when I was ready to leave. You would do this so that I could come in and I still said no, that I thought it was ridiculous and I wanted you to just let me in. Finally, at the end of your rope you told me that if I couldn't have the decency to respect your rules then I was not welcome inside. And then you said, why should I allow you to ruin my new white carpet just because you are so stubborn? With that I became angry and said, okay then I'll see you later when you're not so high minded. Your response was that you were being as kind as you could be, in fact you even offered to take my shoes off for me and put them back on afterwards. But I was so hardheaded I wouldn't take any offer of kindness you gave.

"You see, Christa, that is the way it is with God, He is totally holy in and of Himself and because of that He cannot allow anyone with sin to live with Him in His presence. Our sin would ruin His white carpet (so to speak), which is heaven. A holy God cannot tolerate our sin and allow us to live with Him. It is against His nature and He just cannot accept it. So a sacrifice had to be made to take off our muddy shoes if you will, like the animal killed to clothe Adam and Eve. In Old Testament times, to be accepted before God they sacrificed an animal once a year to atone for their sins. This sacrifice allowed them to come before God just like your offering of taking my shoes off for me. This system of sacrificing animals came to an end when Jesus gave His life on the cross as the Sacrificed Lamb.

"The Bible says, 'He sacrificed for their sins once for all when He offered himself' (Hebrews 7:27). God came down to earth in the form of a man and became our living sacrifice for all time. Jesus's blood was spilt to take away our sins, just like you offered to take my shoes off for me. Jesus went to the same length as you did and said all you have to do is believe on the one whom God sent. But just as I would not allow you to take my shoes off, so the people of the world will not allow Jesus to give them His life because we are spiritually dead, and spiritually dead people need life. If you were to ask the average person if they thought you were being unreasonable about wanting me to take my shoes off they would say, 'no, are you crazy to let someone ruin your white carpet?' They wouldn't allow me to ruin their carpet either. It was not any great demand for you to ask that of me seeing that you had brand-new white carpet in the house. The same is true for God who cannot allow us to live with Him in our sin nature. He is willing to take our shoes off for us in the form of Jesus dying on the cross, so that we would now become holy in God's sight. Not because we were holy, but because He made us that way when we accepted His offering.

"The Bible says: 'Once you were alienated from God and were enemies in your minds because of your evil behavior. But now He has reconciled you by Christ's physical body through death to present you Holy in His sight, without blemish and free from accusation' (Colossians 1:21,22). John the Baptist said when he saw Jesus walking towards him, 'Behold the Lamb of God who takes away the sin of the world' (John 1:29).

"It's kind of like what would happen if people find out about the healing sticks. They would suddenly do anything for one and they would even turn their life around. It's amazing that most people won't turn to God unless they are completely broken and their life is a mess, then they suddenly awaken to their need for Him. What did Jesus ever do to the human race except love us and yet He is the most despised man to ever walk the face of the earth for many people. At the same time He is the most loved man to walk the face of the earth for others. It's incredible how a person responds to Jesus depending on their understanding of Him,'" I explained to Christa.

"Sometimes I feel so sad for people who don't give God the opportunity to love them," Christa said. "If they would only try and give God a chance they would see the love He has and change their life," she told me.

"Like I did," I responded.

"Yes, exactly like you did when you were willing to read and pray again like you did when you were growing up," she quoted.

"All I can say is thank God for bringing me back to Him; can you imagine having this responsibility of the cross without knowing God? I only hope He will give me great wisdom in what to do in the days ahead," I cautioned.

"David," Christa said, "if God helped you find the cross of Jesus Christ then I'm sure He has made a plan for you to do what He wants done with it."

"I only hope you're right, Sis, I hope you're right," I agreed. With that we parted and agreed in our hearts to keep the healings quiet. That time was a special time I kept deep in my heart because God had in two days healed my mother, my sister and me.

# WONDERFUL MIRACLES

The next few weeks I spent time figuring out with family members how large or small a wooden stick had to be in order for a person's body to have a complete healing. When I had it down to my own science, it was time to bring in the big guns, Justin. Justin was our cousin who had been battling cancer for the last few years; he was losing the battle too. He had gotten to the point where he was completely bed ridden. The hard part was to get him to give us a chance. He is in his young twenties and because cancer struck him in his prime he is very angry at the world. He won't let any family come visit him except his immediate family. My sister has tried to go see him, but he refuses, mostly by saying he is too sick to have any visitors. I decided to let the Lord handle Justin and I would get ready for a miracle.

My cola business was going great and I was thankful that trustworthy people were running it. The cross tour was ending in a few days and it would be back in my possession soon. My personal advisor was trying to keep the swarms of media at bay while I was testing the sticks. The general public was getting antsy, because I haven't been giving them much of my attention lately. Overall, I could feel a bubble getting ready to burst. It was like a child blowing up a balloon next to you slowly but surely, and all you can do is sit and watch, waiting for the final blow. The anticipation I felt put butterflies in my stomach. Almost like a three hundred million dollar lottery ticket winner who can't find the ticket. My future was in some kind of limbo, and I wasn't sure if I could handle the days ahead. I didn't think I could ever be holding so much responsibility in my hands.

I prayed every free chance I got. I prayed while driving, walking, sitting, and even sleeping so it seemed. My life was totally dedicated to the Lord of the cross, Jesus, and I was depending on Him for wisdom. I knew that with what I had found out about the healings from the wooden sticks that it would be the most miraculous event to come upon the planet Earth since the time Christ walked in Israel. I knew what people would be capable of if they thought their life could be spared.

I hadn't had any pain since the stick poked me. I knew that pandemonium could break out at the revealing of this great wonder. I could imagine the story in the Bible about the women with the issue of blood, running up behind Jesus and she wasn't going to let anything stop her from getting healed that day. She broke through the crowd of people with sheer determination to just touch the hem of Jesus's garment. When she did she was healed and Jesus honored her faith by acknowledging her. I wondered how Israel would take it, for they had already been making legal claims to the cross lately. All these things were rooted deeply in my mind at what would happen with that old rugged cross of long ago.

# CHAPTER 3
# The Precious Blood of Jesus

I had to do some finagling, but I was able to convince Justin to let me come visit him. When all else failed I simply wrote him a letter and I knew I had a captured audience. I didn't go into too much detail and I never mentioned the cross, I just said things that teetered on the edge of the miraculous and I think he knew he had nothing to lose. He agreed to let me come over. I didn't want to make a spectacle out of the whole thing so I only asked a few family members that already knew about the healing sticks to come with me. The cross was back in my possession now after the tour and this would be the deciding factor of what I would do with the cross if Justin got healed. I had the cross under extremely tight security. Like Fort Knox only the cross has real gold backing it. The streets of heaven are paved with it; God did that to show how important the things that we think make the world go round, to Him He walks on them.

We had about six family members with us when we entered Justin's room. My mother tried to prepare us for what we would see when we went into his room. I don't want to go into detail about what Justin looked like, but he wasn't doing well at all. I approached him with gentleness and he wasn't in very good spirits about the whole thing either. He only agreed to let this happen out of pure desperation and if the healing sticks require some kind of faith on the part of the person they are stuck into to be healed then Justin was without hope. He made it very clear he didn't believe anything would help him. He felt he was in quicksand up to his neck and barely holding on. His faith level on a one to ten scale was at one-half, so if faith had anything to do with his healing we were in trouble.

Mentally he was in just as bad shape as his physical body was. The negative words that came from his mouth kind of threw us off guard and we weren't prepared for it. I understood his attitude and I told him that we came to give him a chance at a new life. I explained that we couldn't guarantee his healing, but if there were any possibility for him to have some kind of hope he should muster up all his faith for what was about to take place. He kind of rambled on about, "Just hurry up already. I don't need a sermon," and so we told him that even though the other healings took place without praying we wanted to pray first anyways to thank God before we started. "Okay," he reluctantly said, "just don't make it last an hour."

"Heavenly Father," I started to pray, "I know you have given us this day to bring your healing power to the world. We pray for the healing of Justin by the power of the blood of Jesus Christ who died on the cross for us and rose from the dead to give us His life everlasting, thank you. In Jesus name, Amen!" With that I instantly plunged the stick from the cross into the arm of a dying man. It went deep into his flesh and he yelled out in pain. His yell sent a chill through my bones like Peter must have felt when he was walking on water and started to sink into the ocean. Jesus let him sink for a minute before he rescued him. Peter started out in good faith then sank because of fear of his surroundings. Was Justin sinking like Peter, would Jesus extend his hand to him and pull him up from this treacherous ocean filled with cancer? These thoughts raced through my mind as though we were in some kind of slow motion Charlie Chapman film. My eyes beheld what was going on as the film being watched scene by scene. Tick-tock went the images and nothing happened. The other healings were instant, but this was not transpiring.

Just then Justin aggressively sat up and threw up all over his bed;

we were all in shock as he sat there looking like he was a ghost. His body went into convulsions; he was shivering like a snowman without a coat. He started throwing up again. He looked as though he could die at any moment. He started to hyperventilate and we quickly got a paper bag and had him breathe into it. After a little while he started to become calm and his face changed to a normal skin tone. As I tried to talk to him he was unresponsive and almost comatose. I asked for something that smelled strong to put under his nose. I was given a bottle of strong-smelling perfume and I waved it under his face. He looked up at me and his eyes seemed to roll back like the red carpet during the Oscars. I thought we lost him at that moment. Then his eyes closed and he went limp. My heart felt like I was going to die myself. All of the sudden he screamed out in a joyous chorus of feeling no more pain. I came out of my freeze frame images and Justin was ecstatic. What seemed like a lifetime finally ended and Justin's mother was crying with great happiness over what just occurred.

"Justin," I said, "talk to us, tell us what happened."

"It, it was very strange," he said in a quivering voice. "You know how they say to pull your lip over your body and swallow yourself up?" he crackled.

"Yes," I answered.

"That's how I felt, like I was being pulled outside in, like going back to being a fetus position all over again and suddenly when I reached that fetus point I exploded back into my body again! That's why I threw up because it was like I was being shot out of a cannon," he shrieked.

"How do you feel now?" I retorted.

"I feel normal and healthy like I used to feel before I got cancer," he responded.

"Do you think you can walk?" I asked.

"I'm sure I can. Let me give it a try, my body feels like I can at least," he quivered.

He moved to the edge of the bed and he put his two legs on the floor and started walking like nothing had ever happened to him. We were exhilarated with amazement when he wildly started jumping all around with his hands raised up into the air. "I don't know who this Jesus is, but I promise from this day on I will give everything I have to Him!" he exclaimed in wild passion.

We all cried tears of great joy at the sight of the most miraculous healing to date for the sticks from the cross. His skin took on its original color again and he was still bald from the chemotherapy, but his eyes gleamed like a baby's eyes opening up for the first time. We had so many questions to ask him, but Justin just said he had dreamed of taking normal showers again for such a long time, he just wanted to take a shower. We told him to go ahead and get himself cleaned up because today was the first day of the rest of his life. While Justin was in the shower, I explained to the family the importance of not yet revealing what happened until I was ready.

I asked Justin's mother to take him to his doctor and tell the doctor that she had been giving him protein foods, and have him checked medically make sure he was completely healed. When Justin came out he looked brand new. He wanted to know everything about who this Jesus was. I told him to start reading the New Testament from the book of Matthew and I gave him a Bible I brought along for the occasion. I told him that as he read the Bible God would reveal Himself to him. I explained how I needed for everything to be legal and that when the time came I would need him for proof that the cross of Jesus Christ through His blood healed him. Justin was willing to do anything I asked, after today. He wanted to go outside and get on his racing bike, but we told him not to overdo it and he said, "Why not? I feel like a new person."

I talked to the family about my plans and again asked for their silence and patience. My world was about to be exposed on a whole new level, and I could only hope that whatever projects were ahead God would see me through.

## POLITICAL HEALING

The next day I met with my advisers who had been with me for a many years. I told them I had an unbelievable phenomenon to reveal to everybody and to gather our inner group the following day for a meeting.

The next day came swiftly for me and I was in deep prayer the night before over how to break the news. Some of the inner groups I met with were lawyers from my firm, others were the scientists and some were clergy that I trusted. I had some of my archeologists from Israel with me. I told the group about the healings that had taken place with the sticks from the cross. There were many questions asked and I informed them this would be a very great time in history for the world. I also explained to them the dangers of what could happen when the general public found out about the cross. I warned them that people would be desperate for a piece of the cross and would go to extreme measures to get their healing. My head of security was there and he suggested that we would have to hire more security personnel to protect it from thieves. I gave my scientists a few pieces from the cross to do their own study of healings, but I warned them to get only people they could absolutely trust for the tests. I put together a timetable of a few days and if the scientists found the same results we would break the news to the world. Of course they picked family members who were in such desperate need they knew if they were healed it was authentic. Our group held the meeting in the strictest confidentiality.

The few days flew by for me and I was running on pure adrenaline by now. The testing the scientists did acted out the same way as my tests worked out and I decided to call the news media to reveal a major announcement concerning the cross. I asked my lawyers to get in contact with my friends in the political arena. I told them I was interested in a very high-ranking government politician who had the very devastating disease of Alzheimer's. He'd had this disease for many years now and I thought if we could get his wife to agree to give the healing sticks a try we would not need any more proof because the world would know if he was healed that it would have to be authentic. For he was famous throughout the entire world and well-known as one of the greatest men in history. His wife agreed and the meeting was set up at his ranch with many doctors there by his side to care for him.

The meeting would be filmed, but not televised unless the results were positive. It seemed there were hundreds of people there that day. Secret Service agents scoured the grounds and checkpoints were set up for all who had permits to enter their property. My own team from my firm was shooting the video to ensure that just in case nothing happened the tape would not be released to the public. I was literally shaking as we entered into the room with this great politician whom I held in great regard. He did not know what was going on and I prayed silently for God's healing power to touch him as we walked towards the couch. His wife was gracious enough to let us try this and I believe she allowed us the chance because of her great love for her husband.

When the time came to actually poke the stick into his arm, I again went into a freeze frame mode like I did with Justin. It was as though clouds suddenly appeared in the room with us; I couldn't speak nor could I ask the others if they could see the clouds in the room. There was a gentle breeze that seemed to sweep the room and with it came an overwhelming peace that filled my being. I heard a voice that spoke to me; whether it was in my mind or spoken out loud I don't know. The voice said: "This is my child and I have come to heal him for all he has given to this world, let my peace rest upon him for the rest of his life!"

I was in a state of astonishment and I looked around to see what everyone else was doing, but their faces were hidden from me. I could just see shadows of the figures of the other people in the room. The whole scenario was surreal and I seemed to be moving in slow motion. The voice of God spoke again saying: "Stick the wood, soaked in the Blood of the Lamb which brings healing to the nations, into the arm of my great servant." With that command I did as the voice told me to do and the room went back into its normal arena again. I could now see everyone and I knew that what I just experienced they knew nothing about. There were no clouds in the room anymore and the crowd of people gasped when I stuck the everlasting healing stick into the arm of that mighty and noble man. I made this stick a little larger than usual because I wanted to be sure a total healing would come.

Later I found this was not necessary for any kind of healing. The sticks only had to be the size of a wooden toothpick to heal a person's body no matter what was wrong with them. His wife cried when she saw the stick stuck in his arm; I felt her pain as I turned and looked at her. Within moments this magnificent man looked into the crowd of people, his eyes swirling like a colored dust storm, and he proclaimed with a loud voice: "What is everyone doing here, is it my birthday or something?"

Everyone in the room went crazy with excitement because they knew that it meant he was able to talk and to comprehend what was going on around him. He looked at his wife and said: "Honey, you know I love you, but you've got to quit throwing me these surprise birthday parties." She threw her arms around him and for the first time in many years he was able to recognize whom she was. Secret Service agents came close around me as if they thought I was some kind of danger to this Ironman politician. They whispered that they needed to see me alone after the crowd of people left.

I was flooded by questions from the crowd and so I told them I would take questions outside to give the family peace after what had just transpired. The family of this great man was so grateful to me for the healing, but I told them not to thank me, but to thank Jesus for it was Him who died on the cross for the healing of the entire world. We were all marveling over the completeness of the healing. It was as though this great man was just asleep and woke up from a nap, for he was perfectly normal in every way. Of course he didn't realize that so much time had passed and he would need some time to get back into the swing of things. I made my way outside to answer questions from the astonished crowd of people gathered at his ranch. Everyone there was startled over what they had witnessed and wanted to know all the facts of what it was they just saw. This questioning went on for some time and finally I had to put an end to it or they would have gone on all day asking me this and that.

The Secret Service agents took me into the house and began to probe me like I was some kind of Albert Einstein. I explained to them what happened and told them that the healing was nothing I did, rather it was from God that the healing took place. They said they would need to get in touch with me again and we departed with that.

I had my staff set up a news conference two days after so that the healing could be confirmed by the doctors to make sure it was really factual. I had written permission to show the whole ordeal on television from the family. The public somehow got hold of the news that a major event happened at the high-ranking politician's house in California and they were clamoring for information. It was like the whole media from around the world was there in the state trying to get a story.

# TELEVANGELIST

The day of the biggest news announcement in history was about to break. First I would tell the story of how I found the cross and I would tell the Gospel of Jesus Christ to the entire world on live television. It was the most remarkable thing that ever happened to me, for I was not the type of person to be able to eloquently speak to large crowds and on live television for that matter. God had promised that He would put the words in our mouths of what to speak in times of great need. He did put words in my mouth because I spoke of the things of God in such a way that I'm sure it melted many millions upon millions of hearts all across the world. I shudder at the thought that God would use such a normal everyday person as myself to proclaim His message of love to the world. It was above me to be able to do this and I knew it was the hand of God on my life for a reason. He wanted to reveal Himself to the world, just as He did in the days of the Prophets of old.

Something big must be about to happen, for since the time that Jesus of Nazareth walked the cities of Israel never had such an event taken place for humankind as this. I was just a lowly businessman who wasn't qualified to take this on, but somehow God moved through me to give me His words to speak and let His named be praised among the nations. I felt so humbled that God would use such a man as myself; it didn't make any sense to me. *Why am I being used, I am not perfect and certainly I am not a saint? Why me?* I wondered. We all have bad things we have done in our lives and maybe have not been as loving and kind to family and friends as we should be, certainly this was me and I was guilty of this, I have to admit, but how could I be chosen for such a monumental task as this? I thought of Jeremiah when he spoke to God and said, "'Ah, Sovereign Lord,' I said, 'I do not know how to speak; I am only a child.' But the Lord said to me, 'Do not say, I am only a child. You must go everywhere I send you to and say whatever I command you'" (Jeremiah 1:6-7).

As I stood before the television cameras I felt great compassion for the world that was watching me through the lenses. I felt the pain and sickness of the disease, starvation, and death that plagued the world. I remembered the images of children with bloated stomachs crying out for food. Somehow it was as though all the downtrodden suffering of mankind was upon me. I knew how Jesus must have felt when He preached to thousands on the hillsides of Israel. I realized that everyone would want a piece of the cross for someone they loved. The magnitude overwhelmed me to the point of breaking down in tears live on television. I felt like Atlas carrying the world on his shoulders. God gave me strength in times when I felt weakness and my mouth moved with words that came from above. The more I spoke the more peace started to fill my being and wonderment at how the Creator of the Universe could actually use me to speak to the masses who were in so much need.

After the news conference was over, I was the most sought after man on the planet. I was provided Secret Service agents by the United States government for my protection. They drove me to places where I had to go in a bulletproof limousine.

The Beatles had nothing over me regarding popularity, but our message was the same, "All you need is love!" I wondered about my future, surely this is not the way I wanted to live my life in the spotlight like some kind of superstar, somehow I was kind of just thrown into all this. I was in way too far over my head. This realization brought me to my knees every chance I got; I prayed that God would guide me in what He wanted me to do. Why didn't he choose Billy Graham or some other powerful man of God? I could not understand. I was a weakling in the kingdom of God. I had not paid my dues as far as time and effort to be qualified for this heavy miraculous journey. But as I read my Bible it talked about King David and how even though he was a sinner God called him a man after His own heart. When I came back to God I did fall in love with Him, for His kindness to not let me go, and it made me realize that He never gave up on me even though I gave up on Him. The more I read, the more I loved and my heart blossomed like a brightly colored flower with petals reaching towards the sky in praise of His mighty name.

It was like a love story between two people who found each other again after many years of being apart. My heart was drawn to God in a way that was more powerful than myself. Each day I longed for our prayer time together. When I didn't have the time to sit alone and pray to my Father, I felt emptiness like lovers feel when they are separated. Sure, I spoke to Him when I drove and everywhere I went, but it was different when I was down on my knees enveloped in His holy presence. I came to realize that it was not about what I did for God or what I gave, money could not buy a relationship with God; it was about my love for Him. He used me because I loved Him with my whole heart! It made me think, *What if all we do in this life has nothing to do with what God actually desires? Our soul winning, preaching and how much money we give. Where we worked or how we lived, what if it is all about our love for God? What if He looks at our love for Him and uses that as His guideline on whether to use us or bless us? What if our heavenly rewards are based on how much we got to know our Heavenly Father intimately and not in our deeds we do for Him? Could we imagine standing before God with all our good works and He is mostly interested in the daily relationship we have with Him alone? How much time we spent in His presence and our knowledge of who He really is?*

The thought was powerful! While most people try to do things to please God and impress Him, I came to realize that what impresses God most is our love for Him! That was it! That was the key, not trying to earn God's favor by witnessing or knocking on doors, not trying to show off in front of other people how spiritual I am. It was only about our desire to want Him, our desire to know about Him and what His personality is like. I thought about how the sheep in a flock would all huddle together. The close sheep saw the shepherd each and every day, so they knew what he looked like, they heard his voice strong and clear. The sheep that were far away from the shepherd merely followed the other sheep in front of them. They didn't know what the shepherd looked like, they didn't see personal things about him like the sheep who were close did. All they saw were the backs of the other sheep in front of them. Wherever these sheep went the tailgater sheep followed.

What kind of sheep was I? Did I follow close or was I just a follower of others? Would my reward be because I tried to be a good person or would it be because I loved God with all my heart? Did I know His voice, His word, and His personality? All that other stuff is meaningless unless we have an honest love for God, a love that takes the time to talk with Him and relate to Him, like a husband and wife do together. The Bible says, "For this reason a man will leave his father and mother and be united to his wife, and the two will become one flesh. This is a profound mystery, but I am talking about Christ and the church" (Ephesians 5:31-32).

Here the Apostle Paul was talking about husbands and wives and suddenly he relates their relationship together as the relationship with Christ and the Church! God thinks of us as His bride and a bride gets to know her husband by spending time with him, not once a week in church or reading a Christian book that entertains you. This opened up a whole new meaning for me and I think it is why after two thousand years nobody else was able to find the cross. God chose me out of all the great men to walk the earth. He chose the simplicity of a weak man who had a strong heart for Him. Jesus died for us because He loved us and He allowed me to find the cross because He knew beforehand that my heart would be filled with such great love for Him that is hard to put into words. When it came right down to it, I was madly in love with God! God was looking for companionship; He created the human race so we would come to love Him for His kindness to us. Our hearts are hardened to the point where we don't want it to be that easy, we want to have to do something for Him. All God wants us to do is receive Him and in return love Him back for the love He gave us! The rest of work we do will take care of itself in time.

This revelation was a huge breakthrough for me and I was humbled to be able to understand that God wants our hearts, not our money or our good works. The other things we do to help the kingdom of God grow will follow when our hearts are in love with God. This may be the secret to the universe and a lot of people are so busy trying to impress God they have lost what is most important with Him and that is He wants our love, He wants our companionship!

# CHAPTER 4
# A Carpenter's Dream

My life became the world's; everywhere I went the news media followed. It came to the point where I couldn't walk around and be myself anymore. The pressure was getting to me and after the revelation that a piece of the cross healed the most respected political personality of the modern world, everybody wanted a piece of it. Israel had filed a lawsuit against me claiming that the cross belonged to them because it came from their country. They have been in a terrible uprising with the Palestinian extremists who chose to take the path of homicide bombings to try to get what they felt was right. Israel has lost many good soldiers searching out the terrorists, and many innocent men, women, and children have been killed by murderers. They fill their bombs with nails and steel balls to cause the most damage they can possibly inflict. Many innocent people have been maimed for life. Children without legs, women without arms, and many crippled as a result of the most despicable acts of terrorism any human being could ever imagine. It was animalistic to try to solve problems by the killing of innocent civilians.

My heart grieved for the people of Israel and also the innocent Palestinian people who wanted no part of these vicious attacks. I knew Israel could use the healing sticks to help the wounded people of their nation. I hoped and prayed that the Palestinian people would come to their senses and realize that their leader was taking them down a path of destruction. I prayed for the leaders also, that they would seek a peaceful means to work things out instead of they way they were trying to accomplish their goals. I believe that if the Palestinians would try the path that Martin Luther King Jr. did they would be more successful. His nonviolent tactics formed the foundation of what he sought to bring about. I have the utmost respect for Dr. King and I think he ranks up there as one of the greatest men to ever walk on the face of the planet Earth.

The American government wanted the cross for their own special reasons and the scientists wanted it to do their own scientific experiments with it. I felt like a man whose hands and feet were tied between two horses and the horses whipped to run in opposite directions. I was literally being pulled apart; the world that had loved me now wanted me for their own agenda. I had death threats on my life and I felt like a fox with bloodhounds barking at his heels.

I decided to have meetings with my close-knit advisers, which also included American and Israeli government officials. We talked about the cross and what should be done with it. Should it be left alone as a historical relic or would Israel's lawsuit take it from me? My lawyers were battling for legal ownership of the cross with Israel. They allowed me to take it and now that the healings had happened they wanted it back. All this was discussed and I felt like I really didn't know what to do with that old rugged cross.

My days were filled with turmoil and my nights with sleeplessness. For a few weeks it seemed like my relationship with God was being determined over my decision of what to do with the historic relic. My confusion was incredible, kind of like on the Resurrection Day of Jesus when we celebrate with Easter bunnies and eggs. What on earth does that have to do with Jesus rising from the dead? Well, maybe my confusion was not comparable to the world's regarding Easter, but I needed time alone to figure it out.

I told the group I needed a few days to be alone and decide what would be best for the world and what would be fair. They agreed and I went to my mother's house to visit for a while. It was great to get home-cooked meals again; my mother was like a newborn spring chicken after her healing. Busy as a bee, gliding around her kitchen singing and trying to cook and bake goodies for me to enjoy. I must have gained a few pounds my first day home. Mother was always talking about me going out with Tracy and had matchmaking schemes going on all the time for us to get together.

Mother had a basement where I made myself a prayer room to be alone in. Mom knew of the important decisions I was facing and she would always say, "Son, it is in God's hands, just listen for His voice."

The first night I prayed came and went with no answer from the Lord. I prayed and read my Bible hour after hour; I was seeking out God's will for the cross, but without response. The second night was without any answer either. On the third day of the third night I put a blanket over my head and in prayer to God I said: "Lord, this is my sackcloth, please tell me what you want me to do with the cross?" I was surprised at the answer that spoke gently to my mind, the reply said: "Go to sleep and rest, don't worry about tomorrow for tomorrow will worry about itself!" I knew that was actually a Bible verse in the book of Matthew 6:34. By that time I was exhausted anyways, so I obeyed out of pure fatigue. Normally I would have tried to figure out if it was God speaking or just my mind making something up. I didn't feel some great spiritual power when the thought came for me to go to sleep. But when all else fails just do what your body tells you and mine was telling me to get into bed.

I slept like an angel on a cloud flowing over the earth in harmony with the world. Suddenly, I dreamed I was sitting before a judge with long white hair looking like one of those old movies and he was asking me what I did with the cross. I was dreaming I knew, but it seemed as though I were really in a heavenly courtroom. The judge hammered down his anvil and demanded from me, "What did you do with the cross?"

"I don't know, your honor," I stammered. "I didn't know what to do with it and so I was praying and asking God to tell me what to do."

"Did God then tell you what to do with the cross?" the judge asked.

"No, He didn't, your honor," I replied.

"Well then, son of man, you have found favor in the sight of the

Lord God Almighty. Therefore, I will instruct you in what you are to do with the cross," he thundered boldly.

"I will heed your advice, your honor, let not your words depart from my mind," I trembled.

"Listen carefully," he instructed. "Take a small piece of the cross and give it to the scientists for study, do you understand me?" he asserted.

"Yes, sir, I understand," I quivered.

"This piece shall not be just any piece, but it shall be the piece in the center of the cross. It is to be twelve inches long to confirm to the Twelve Tribes of Israel to show them that Jesus is their Messiah and has come to heal their land!" he commanded. "Then take the remaining pieces and cut them up into toothpick-size healing sticks to heal the blind, sick, and diseased of the world. These sticks are to be forty-sixteenths long and have the thickness of three thirty-seconds. Every stick is to be treated with the utmost care, for it is through the blood that soaked into the wood on the cross that Jesus Christ, the Lord of Heaven and Earth, hung on between the two worlds when He gave His life for the all of mankind. Even the dust from the sticks is to be collected for later use, as instructions will be given to you, oh most favored one. Listen to what the Spirit says unto you!" he thundered.

I was in a state of extreme weakness by then, all I could do was bow my knee and sit attentively.

"Take the healing sticks and give my children of Israel half of all the sticks you collect and divide the remaining sticks as you wish. For you have been found to be trustworthy before the Lord of Hosts and it is His good pleasure to entrust you with what you feel is fair among your people. Now go and do as you have been instructed for the time of the end is soon," he instructed.

"I will do as you have said, your honor," and with that I awakened in a semi-sleep, fully aware of my instructions. However, I wasn't sure if what happened to me was a dream or if I really was translated into glory. If it was only a dream then my dreams should be made into Hollywood movies, because this one was extraordinary. My heart seemed to be warmed and my spirit quieted, and I went back into a nice sound sleep.

# BLUEPRINT SPECIFICATIONS

The next morning I awakened with a sense that I knew all along what I was going to do with the cross. It was kind of like my dream, vision or visit to heaven—whatever it was that happened to me—was implanted in my mind as my own thoughts. With my plan intact, I knew I had a lot of work set out ahead of me.

Mom cooked the most superb breakfast for me and I told her of my plans and how I got them. She understood because she has always been the kind of women that seemed to know what God wanted and how we should do as He says. I left and started my mission with a vengeance. I had my firm order brand-new equipment that the toothpick companies use to make toothpicks. I set up a state-of-the-art manufacturing center in the lab where the cross was. It was set up kind of like a clean room where microchips are made, only we enclosed it in an atmosphere to not let any dust escape the area, for even the dust has value. I was reminded of the women who asked Jesus to heal her daughter from demon possession and she said to the Lord, "Even the dogs eat the crumbs that fall from their master's table." Jesus responded by granting her request and her daughter was healed that very hour. (Matthew 15:27,28). These crumbs were the dust that was to come when the wood from the cross was cut into healing sticks.

My team brought in wood-cutting experts, and after the whole team agreed on how we were going to do the production, the work of God began. The compounds were so secure that even the workers had to go through several chambers just to get in and go out. Even x-ray machines were set in place for this incredible event about to take place. My lawyers had spoken with the Israeli government and they agreed on the solution to split the sticks with them. Their one request was to be allowed to send over a team of experts to make sure everything was done in the most perfect way. I agreed that this would be all right and so the process was in full swing.

When the experts from Israel arrived, they brought with them a soldier who had gotten his left leg blown off when a homicide bomber exploded himself in a crowded hotel. When security and the soldiers ran in to help this man, a second terrorist blew himself up and the soldier had his leg blown off. He was highly honored by the Israeli government, for even after his injury he was able to shoot another homicide bomber that was waiting outside the hotel for people to flee.

They asked me if they could have a stick before we started to cut them up to help the soldier. He was walking with a wooden leg and so I told him to sit down and that I was honored to be able to give him a stick. He lifted his pant leg and rolled it up to below the knee where the wooden leg attached. I kneeled down to the soldier's feet while he took the wooden leg off. I looked up at him with great compassion in my eyes and told him that his leg would he back as normal because Jesus Christ the Savior of Israel and the world came down to earth and died on the cross for his salvation. I asked him if he was waiting for the Messiah to come back to save Israel and he said, "Yes, I wait every day for that blessed hope." I told him that the Messiah did come to save Israel two thousand years ago and He was crucified on the cross that I was about to stick into his body. I asked him, "If your leg grows back as normal, will you then believe in Jesus as the Messiah?"

He spoke humbly and said, "Only God could bring this kind of healing, so if I am healed I will forever believe Jesus Christ to be my Messiah and King."

I told his buddies that came with them that the God of Abraham, Isaac and Jacob was about to do a great miracle right before their very eyes. I told them that on this cross hung their Messiah and now it was time for them to receive Him and believe. I then had the soldier roll down his pants over the amputated leg.

"Okay," I said, "roll up your other pant leg and close your eyes." The soldier closed his eyes tightly as if he were going to be shot or something. I said, "God brought you here today so you may believe that your Messiah is filled with compassion for you."

I took the stick and thrust it into the calf of his other leg; he barely flinched at the pain. I knew the Israeli soldiers were tough as nails and he opened his eyes as his other pant leg started to wiggle.

"I'm feeling something happening," he shouted and suddenly within an instant there was another foot sticking outside his pants.

The group's eyes flashed like light bulbs during an Academy Awards preview. He stood up and jumped with great joy and he started speaking his native language and praising God for his healing. He ran over to me and hugged me, almost breaking my back because of his excitement.

With tears streaming down his face, he dropped to his knees and said: "I will forever worship my Messiah Jesus Christ who came for my healing. What must I do to be clean in His sight?" he begged.

I asked him to repeat what I said in prayer and I was astonished as I heard the prayers of the whole group of Israeli men that came with him come to the Lord Jesus Christ that day. My life couldn't have been more fulfilled that day as I wondered what kind of effect this would have on the Jewish people of Israel. The group's lives were transformed the instant they witnessed the growing back of the leg of the soldier. I burst out laughing as I asked the soldier if he thought his other shoe would fit.

The entire group then burst out laughing together. "I don't know, I may have to go to the shoe store today!" he exclaimed in great joy. His face was beaming like the bright morning star. I told the group, which included master wood workers from Israel, that their Messiah was indeed a carpenter too.

We took a break because the lab was filled with brilliant ecumenism. Firstly, because the soldier was healed, and secondly, because a son of Israel had returned to his Messiah and many in the group there were Christians. Later on, the first piece was cut for the scientific world to study. Next came the cutting up of the cross for the toothpick-size sticks. You would have thought that we were all there watching a heart transplant or something; the people inside the lab became as quiet as lab mice when the first piece of the cross went into the machine. The machines were set to the specifications I had given them. Each piece was to be specially wrapped just like a toothpick except this wrapping was stronger to prevent breakage and made of exceptional material to keep the healing sticks preserved. The tips of the sticks were to be sharpened so fine that it would not take much effort for them to pierce the skin. My mind exotically thought about this scripture in the Old Testament: *"And I will pour out on the house of David and the inhabitants of Jerusalem a spirit of grace and supplication. They will look on me, the one they have pierced, and they will mourn for him as one mourns for an only child, and grieve bitterly for him as one grieves for a firstborn son"* (Zechariah *12:10).* At that time it seemed to me that this was the vehicle that God would use to tell His people of Israel that He longed for them to come home.

The CIA, FBI, and Secret Service from the U.S. and Israel were there to make sure everything was kosher. I had expert cameramen set up with views on every angle to document the cutting up of the cross. Even the soldier's leg was shown in its amputated state and after the new leg grew back we filmed the event when the soldier lifted his pants to see his brand-new leg.

The news media was demanding to know what was taking place inside the lab. The Israeli government asked us not to expose the healing of the soldier to the public yet and so everyone in the building gave his or her promise to keep it a secret for now. We had a tight group working in the lab and they were all very professional and knew the great consequences of what we had on our hands. When the sticks were all cut up and wrapped, there were over three million sticks. This process took seven days to do because I made sure it was done as professionally as possible; I spared no expense as God spared no expense for us by sending His only Son. The American government made sure they took some sticks that day to ensure that if something ever happened to an American President he would be protected.

These sticks were more valuable than anything in the history of the world. As our days wrapped up, we had to have police escorts allow us to drive out of the complex because news media were there from around the world waiting for any piece of information they could get their hands on. I had my firm's press secretary give them the update while I slipped out in a different car that nobody knew I had. My life became so hunted that I had to use many different vehicles just to get around unnoticed. Even though I had Secret Service agents guarding me, every once in a while I still liked to drive myself and not be transported by their limousine.

# VIOLENCE ERUPTS

The world became crazy over the cross; some people protested and marched in the streets because the cross was cut up into small pieces. They thought it was defaming God and that God would judge America for it. Other groups banded together to try to force the government to stop the healing sticks from being spread around the world. These groups were anti-God and were afraid that the whole world would turn to believe in Jesus as the Savior. They took on violent forms and turned to terrorist-type tactics to get the American government to put an end to what they called the greatest deception of all time. They were frightened that if people saw the miracles happen then they would be forced to have to make a decision regarding the truth of the Bible. There was violence in some other countries over what we did with massive street protests and the burning of buildings in foreign countries. They marched, they ranted and raved, and the upheaval was tremendous. Some countries branded America and me as anti-religious nuts.

Different religions that didn't believe in Jesus were saying the healings were fixed and the whole thing was a religious scandal to try and make their religion look false. Normal religions that were once laidback had now become more militant in the ways they took action to stop the so-called deceptions. Even some mainstream American churches were mad at the thought of the actual cross of Jesus Christ being cut up into splinters. They wanted it preserved as a holy museum piece. They had filed federal lawsuits to try to stop the cross from being cut up, but they never succeeded in their endeavors. The enemies of Israel were up in arms over the thought that Israel now had some new kind of weapon where their soldiers wouldn't die. They feared Israel would now go to war against them because of this new weapon that America and Israel had concocted. Their armies were placed on high alert and masses of soldiers guarded the borders between countries. The world was in utter chaos over the events. It surely seemed to be the last days that Jesus spoke of before His coming.

On the other hand, many other churches praised the cutting up of the cross for they said it would prove that Jesus was the Christ and that He was God come down to earth in the flesh to die for the sins of the whole world. The atheists were experiencing migraine headaches as never before and the evolutionists were denying the whole thing as a hoax. Bumpers stickers across America said things like: "Jesus Christ wood heal you" and "God wood save you" and "The cross = the missing link!" Talk shows had nothing else more important than the cross to discuss; their phone lines were jammed with nonstop callers discussing the events of what had taken place all over the world. Television now seemed to be like a 24-hour talk show also, with experts and clergymen all weighing in on the miracle of the cross. The images of the healing of the great politician flashed the television screens in earnest as though the days were short. Other healings had been televised and the public was in great enthusiasm over seeing these miracles over and over again.

It was very strange to see the nations of the earth talking about Jesus Christ all at once, nonstop over the issue of the cross. Jesus had taken the entire world by storm and certainly His gospel was reaching even the most remote places around the globe. The gospel was being preached to every man, women and child! The grandest thing was it was being done by the secular media and all for free. God had taken the devil's stronghold and was using it for His glory. Some of my media programs that I put out were making extraordinary amounts of money and it was all going to the Christian feeding ministries that help stop hunger worldwide. It benefitted millions of suffering people more than ever before in the history of the earth. The people of the world were reaping the benefits of my programs that I was charging the media to use. Hunger was beginning to become more extinct than ever before.

Revival was breaking out in churches all over the world. It was an unprecedented revival that was sweeping through like a hurricane throughout the nations. In American, churches the flood gates were opened and the churches were so filled up that in most major cities Christian churches had to rent their city's sporting arenas to allow all the people in who wanted to go to church. The scene was absolutely amazing; God's Spirit was being poured out on all flesh. There was no denying it. Even the skeptics gave in to what was happening and acknowledged that it must be something from God. There were many reports of healings taking place even without the sticks. People's faith in what they saw over and over again at the ranch where a great man was healed made their own faith flourish.

Not only were Christian churches experiencing revival, the Catholic churches worldwide experienced revival as never seen before in the history of the world. Movie stars weren't movie stars anymore, now Jesus Christ was superstar. People didn't care that movie stars were being married for the seventh time. In fact, the Hollywood stars were losing an enormous amount of money because the public only wanted to see the events of the many healings that were taking place, so they were not playing the weekly television lineup. The public clamored for anything on television that had to do with a man of God speaking on the subject. It was nonstop Jesus; you could almost hear the rocks and the trees crying out for their redemption.

What a time to be alive, what a time to know and love the Savior of the world. I was ecstatic at what was going on worldwide. Bookstores were sold out of Bibles; they could not keep them on the selves. People who owned many Bibles even sold them on street markets for a lot of money. The Bible had become the most sought after book ever. Church donations poured in and Christian television stations were buying many of the major networks around America and the world. It was real revival across the globe; some thought it was heaven coming down to earth. Others thought we were in the millennium. The people who believed in aliens were proclaiming that I came down from a spaceship and was a space alien. I had to humble myself before God so that I would not get a big head over what was being said about me. Some were proclaiming me as the Messiah; some thought I was the Savior that was to come. Others hated me bitterly for their own reasons of disbelief, jealousy or whatever; I had become the most loved and hated man in the world for giving out the many sticks that I did and the miracles that flashed across the screens became ingrained in the minds of the general public. Such things were not ever seen before by mankind.

## GODS OF MEN

There were very organized rings that tried to get the healing sticks for their own. I had the sticks placed under government protection because they were the most sought after commodity on the planet. I received millions of letters asking me for a stick for cancer patients, car accident victims, liver diseases, and many other things that people were dying from. Millionaires were offering tens of millions of dollars for the sticks. People would bow down to me when they saw me and it was unsettling to me because I wanted them to bow down before God, not me.

The same thing happened to Paul and Barnabas when God was using them and people were being healed. The people began to say they were gods come down to them in human form. When Paul and Barnabas heard of this, they tore their clothes and rushed out into the crowd shouting: "'Men, why are you doing this? We too are only men, human like you. We are bringing you good news'"(Acts 14:14,15). I didn't want anybody to worship me, and I had to keep making it known that what was happening was not from me, but rather it was from God Himself.

I asked some of the local churches if I could speak in televised services to make sure everybody knew where I was coming from. I was given permission to do so and my first church service was broadcast around the world on live television. My speech went something like this: "Dear people of the world, I want you to know that I am not a God, nor am I an angel or the Savior of the world. I am just a regular person, David Clayton, whom God used to bring His healing and His word to you, the people of this world. God did this miraculous event so that you would believe in His son Jesus Christ. He did this as a way to prove that He is the Lord Almighty and that He loves you with all His heart. He sent this as a way to prove that Jesus Christ was the Savior of the world and that He rose again from the grave where now He sits at the right hand of God. God sent His Son two thousand years ago, now He sends His cross to show the world once and for all that Jesus is the Lord of all and He wants you to give your hearts to Him. He is calling you unto Himself; He wants to save you so that you can live in heaven with Him someday. This may be the last sign He gives before His return and so the choice is up to you. Will you believe or will you still harden your hearts to the love that God has poured out for you? This day do not harden your hearts to God, but be filled with His Holy Spirit and accept His life within you. Peter stood up and proclaimed to the crowd what the Prophet Joel wrote: 'In the last days, God says, I will pour out my Spirit on all people. You sons and daughters will prophesy, your young men will see visions, your old men will dream dreams' (Acts 2:17). Then he continues with, 'And everyone who calls on the name of the Lord will be saved' (Acts 2:21). This may be the exact time nearing the return of Jesus Christ for His Church, please do not miss out on the greatest event to ever take place on the planet Earth, which is the Rapture of the Church.

"The life of Christ saves you, for you were born spiritually dead in sin, but because Jesus lives He will give you His life and that is life eternal. It is not the death of Christ that saves you alone, it is His resurrected life and His life is freely given to all who ask. For once you were born spiritually dead, but now you can be born again spiritually alive. You have been transformed from death to life. Please don't go on without giving yourself a chance at having this brand-new life. You can be born all over again to a fresh new start, behold the old will pass away and the new will come. If we as a world will come to God He will heal our lands. That is my prayer for you, that you will come to know a God who gave His all to show His incredible love for you.

"I know that many people on the verge of death need the sticks, but there are only a limited number of sticks and not merely enough for the needs of America and the world. Because of this I have come to a conclusion that the sticks will be used for the people whose lives are nearing death for whatever reason that is. Still there are too many people in this condition than there are sticks. I have decided that the public, if you have a family member in this condition, please fill out a form for consideration for a stick. When we confirm that the requests are legitimate we will then hold a lottery type picking for the healing sticks. Each state will hold its own lottery and a government panel will oversee the distribution of the sticks from that point on. Some sticks will be given to other countries of the world as well.

"This is the only fair way to do this because the needs are so enormous. If I were to sell the sticks only the extremely rich would get them. From the example that Jesus gave, I have to let all people have a chance even if they are poor. Many may not like this, many may disapprove, but what other way could I do this and be fair to everyone? I am sure that in each state you will see the healings of people in desperate need and be able to rejoice with me that God has sent down to earth His healing power in the form of His holy cross, on which He gave His life for you. The forms can be downloaded on your computer at **www.jesuswoodheals.com** and this program of goodwill toward men will try to be done as fast as possible so please we ask that anyone not tie up the system with false information about your health. This will only make this take longer and people may die who are in desperate need. So I ask you to reach down into your hearts and let's all work together on bring the healing power of God to our world. I pray that God would bless each and every one of you with good health and peace. May God bless you all!"

# CHAPTER 5
# O Jerusalem, Jerusalem

The next few months were hard on me personally. I did talk shows, television appearances and even went to the White House and other major political places. Some days were really rough for me; there were times when I felt like I was walking through quicksand or molasses and other days of great joy and excitement. Israel had taken their sticks and set up a similar type system to help their citizens and military. As a good gesture they gave away ten percent of their sticks to their Muslim neighboring nations as an olive branch of peace. The United States did the same and gave sticks to other nations to show Jesus's compassion to all humanity.

Reports from other countries saw an explosion of healings even without the sticks by people who witnessed healings and had great faith in God themselves. The number of healings without the sticks far outnumbered healings from the sticks in many third-world countries as revival spread like hot lava boiling down a mountainside. Israel was extremely thankful for the sticks, but after they had some healings put live on television this caused a real uproar for those who did not believe in Jesus as their Messiah. Some said, "If Jesus is not the Messiah then how could these healings be taking place?" Others said, "It was miraculous, but it had nothing to do with Jesus." The same things were said to Jesus during the time He walked the streets of Israel. Even after healing blind people, lame people, and raising people from the dead they still asked for a sign from heaven. How much does it take for some people to believe? So the same thing was going on in modern Israel now as was in the days of Jesus then.

Others had done their own investigations and proved that the cross was dated for the time in which historically Jesus was crucified, so Israel was in a real pickle internally. Though they gratefully received the sticks, they were divided because of religious reasons.

As I read the book of Isaiah I was amazed at the fact that the Messiah of Israel was spoken about so many times and yet so many Jewish people never came to see that Jesus was their Messiah. Isaiah says, "Who has believed our message and to whom has the arm of the Lord been revealed? He grew up before him like a tender shoot, and like a root out of dry ground. He had no beauty or majesty to attract us to him, nothing in his appearance that we should desire him. He was despised and rejected by men, a man of sorrows, and familiar with suffering. Like one from whom men hide their faces he was despised, and we esteemed him not.

"Surely he took up our infirmities and carried our sorrows, yet we considered him stricken by God, smitten by him, and afflicted. But he was pierced for our transgressions, he was crushed for our iniquities; the punishment that brought peace was upon him, and by his wounds we are healed" (Isaiah 53:1-5). It goes on to say more things and yet this was written seven hundred and forty years before Jesus was even born. David wrote in Psalms, "Dogs have surrounded me; a band of evil men has encircled me, they have pierced my hands and my feet. I can count all my bones; people stare and gloat over me. They divide my garments among them and cast lots for my clothing" (Psalm 22:16-18).

My heart thundered in sorrow as I read again in Isaiah, "Therefore the Lord himself will give you a sign: The virgin will be with child and will give birth to a son, and will call him Immanuel" (Isaiah 7:14). How much clearer does God have to make it and then He even announces His birthplace, "But you, Bethlehem Ephrathah, though you are small among the clans of Judah, out of you will come for me one who will be ruler over Israel, whose origins are from old, from ancient times" (Micah 5:2).

I remembered to the time when Jesus rode into Jerusalem on a donkey and God foretold the distinguished event in the Old Testament also, "Rejoice greatly, O Daughter of Zion! Shout, Daughter of Jerusalem! See, your king comes to you, righteous and having salvation, gentle and riding on a donkey, on a colt, the foal of a donkey" (Zechariah 9:9). Again Zechariah explains Jesus's crucifixion when he says, "If someone asks him, 'What are these wounds on your body?' He will answer, 'The wounds I was given at the house of my friends'" (Zechariah 13:6). My heart broke for the people of Israel how that after so many scriptures concerning their Messiah that were written hundreds and thousands of years before why they still refused to recognize Jesus as the coming king. I read that Paul the Apostle said, "Even to this day when Moses is read, a veil covers their hearts. But, whenever anyone turns to the Lord, the veil is taken away" (2 Corinthians 3:15,16). That was the answer for this tiny nation under distress from its enemies. God will always deliver anyone who calls on His name and the people of Israel just weren't calling out. My spirit within me grieved for the nation of Israel.

# MY PERSONAL DOCUMENTARY

This is part of my life's story where the man came up to my front yard with a gun in his hand and demanded a stick. He was shot by security and then instantly healed when I poked a healing stick into him. The scene was incredible and I was just as stunned as everyone else was. My life was spared that day and because of that I wanted to make sure everything that has happened since the day I found the cross was documented and told truthfully. That is why I am writing this personal documentary so these miracles will be part of an accurate historical record. I do not want any part of this most astonishing time in history to be written in error. So this is my personal account written by my own hand.

I decided to go back to Israel because the people there were inviting me with all their hearts to return to that great country. I was treated with royalty when I arrived and I could tell they were grateful, but I had to explain to them it was not me who brought them this great healing it was their Messiah, Jesus. They knew I would say things like this about Jesus in public and they received it with open arms, at least most of them. Others criticized me for the remarks I made and said I was a fanatic.

The country was in a terrible crisis because of the terrorist homicide bombings by Palestinian militants and extremists. I visited hospitals where innocent women and children were in critical condition just because on a certain day they ate lunch in a restaurant and happened to be at the wrong place at the wrong time. How could any human ever think to kill this way would be acceptable to God? It is a mind-boggling realization that this is taught to young children instead of reading, writing, and arithmetic in schools.

The people in America were still in shock over the September 11, 2001, terrorist attack on the World Trade Centers and the Pentagon. The terrorists flew passenger airplanes into the buildings, which caused thousands of innocent people's lives. The ruthless murders were a tragedy for our nation and the country of Israel understood completely because every day for them is September 11th. The people in Israel understood that they must take care of each other because they were all in the same predicament. They were like one large body who when one suffers they all suffer. The country was in agony badly and not just from terrorist attacks alone, but from a weakened economy because of lack of tourism. They usually had about $2.3 billion a year coming into Israel, but now people were afraid to travel there, so the economy was in dire need and they were hurting really bad. About half of their tourist shops have shut down and the hotel industry has only about 25 percent of the rooms occupied.

One visitor told me of a story when he was coming to Israel to visit his Jewish friends. They gave him money and told him wherever he went in Israel use the extra money to pay double your bill to try to help the economy of that beautiful nation. It is Jewish law for the leaders of the community to be responsible for the needs of the poor, but it has been the generous giving of Jewish and Christian people from around the world that has helped them to survive this time of crisis in their history. Still they are suffering from what has been done to their country as a result of terrorism. The Christians in America have banded with the people of Israel to show them that we support them and would stand by them in their greatest hour of need. Televised church services held tribute to the tiny country of Israel that has less than one percent of the total amount of land in the Middle East region. When you consider that the Muslim and Arab nations own ninety-nine percent of the land in the Middle East it is ridiculous to think that they want to own tiny Israel too.

# JESUS WEPT

I was reminded about the verses in the Bible in which Jesus said: "O Jerusalem, Jerusalem, you who kill the prophets and stone those sent to you, how often I have longed to gather your children together, as a hen gathers her chicks under her wings, but you were not willing. Look, your house is left to you desolate. For I tell you, you will not see me again until you say, 'Blessed is he who comes in the name of the Lord'" (Matthew 23:37-39). Israel is the apple of God's eye and He longs for them to come to Him for salvation. Jesus loved the city of Jerusalem and when He saw the city, He wept over it and said: "If you, even you had only known on this day what would bring you peace, but now it is hidden from your eyes. The days will come upon you when your enemies will build an embankment against you and encircle you and hem you in on every side. They will dash you to the ground, you and your children within the walls. They will not leave one stone on another, because you did not recognize the time of God's coming to you" (Luke 19:41-44). It seems rather prophetic that this scripture mentions walls when Israel is in the process of building walls around her to try to stop terrorists from coming in. Also Jesus said: "A time is coming when anyone who kills you will think he is offering a service to God" (John 16:2). The signs of terrorists blowing themselves up fulfill this scripture accurately. The terrorists believe that killing women and children will bless them for eternity when they become a martyr. I was hoping that the healing sticks would be the opening of the Jewish people's eyes for their Messiah, Jesus.

I heard the "Legend of the Dogwood Tree"; this is a legend and not fact, but it is rather interesting. The story goes that during the time of Christ this tree was a huge strong tree that they used as the wood for crucifixions. Because the tree felt remorse for its chosen purpose and felt repentant, Jesus said to the tree as He was being nailed to it that never again would it have to bear the anguish of being used for such evil. So Jesus said from now on the dogwood tree would grow bent and twisted and be very slender. The flowers of the tree would form a cross and in the center there would be something like nail prints—brown rust and stained red. In the center would be the crown of thorns so that everybody would remember what took place on that tree. The legend shows the compassion Jesus had for everything involved in humanity. When I think of Jesus I think how up to date He is with each of us individually. Though millions of people come from different races and cultural backgrounds, each person is able to relate to God in love and understanding. That reflection always makes me realize that Jesus is the fulfillment that every human being needs in his or her life and that is what everybody needs rather than the things the world has offered as replacements.

# CHAPTER 6
# False Prophets

Many things were happening that weighed heavily on my heart. We had just had some bombs explode in American shrines over the hotly debated healings that were going on. These groups of radicals were trying to stop the revival that was overtaking the nation. Some churches had been targeted by the groups, but thank God no one had been killed as of yet. My present time was one of great happiness and sorrow. I saw things that were never seen before and my heart rejoiced in them. As with all things that are great comes things that will also bring us down. I was aware that with the responsibility I had been given I would also suffer through certain aspects of it.

I was invited to speak at a pre-arranged healing, where a man who had been blessed got his healing stick and they were going to show it on the local television stations. Tracy, my assistant, was accompanying me as she usually does. This man was in horrible shape physically. He was in desperate need for a liver transplant and wasn't expected to live for more than a few days. His time of receiving his stick was certainly strategic. The broadcast would be live from the hospital where he was being cared for.

I arrived in my Leer jet early enough to have a nice breakfast and relax a little before driving to the hospital with Tracy. The personal director of the hospital came to my hotel room and briefed Tracy and I on what was going to take place and all the other stuff we were going to do. I had been to many of these appearances where I showed up to give a person my encouragement. The situations were all about the same, but each person was an individual that God loved. For the people who were getting healed it was a major event in their life. I treated each such visitation, as it was God's love being poured out so my life was enriched just to be a part of them.

We drove into the hospital on this particularly warm day. The sun was bright, my heart was warm, and I seemed to be in a kind of lackadaisical mood. Inside the hospital room I met with the patient and we shook hands as we greeted each other. He was filled with great anticipation in what was ahead. The cameras were rolling and his wife was going to be the person to poke him with the stick. He closed his eyes as if he were a small child getting ready for a shot in the arm at school.

"One, two, three," his wife counted and she poked him in the upper arm. The crowded room burst into great joy and clapped as the stick thrust into his flesh. But this somehow did not go like the other healings I had witnessed. The man did not return to his normal skin tone and he seemed to be still in his weakened condition. His wife was very nervous and asked me if maybe she poked the stick in wrong. I said no that she did just fine. We all stood there in amazement with television cameras rolling. Most people in America by now had seen many of these healing too, and so they knew something was wrong as much as we did. My skin crawled within me and I asked, "Scott, how do you feel?"

"Not very good," he answered feebly.

"Are you in pain right now?" I stammered back.

"Yes, my pain is always very severe and it hasn't changed any since the stick went in," he replied.

"I am not sure what happened to you, but I promise you I will find out, so please try to relax and we will check to see what is going on okay," I said softly.

"Yes, sir," he kind of grumbled.

We all walked out of the room and immediately I was bombarded with questions of what happened. "I do not know what happened, I don't understand it either," I told the group. "Please give me the healing stick and I will check it to see why Scott didn't get healed."

Scott's wife came out of the room in tears of sorrow. She was wailing in grief. "David," she sobbed, "why, why didn't my husband get healed?"

I put my arms around her and explained, "I really don't know what on earth is going on, but I promise you that I will find out quickly."

"Do you have any other healing sticks with you?" she cried.

"No, I had to quit carrying them with me after a man tried to shoot me for a stick. It's the only way I can protect myself from people trying to get sticks from me by violence," I explained.

"What are we going to do? My husband is dying," she appealed.

"Please be patient and I will go right now to find out what happened. Do you have the stick with you?" I asked her.

She handed me the stick and I asked the doctors what his prognosis was. The head doctor said he was expected to die within a few days if nothing happened. "Here, take my cell phone number and call if his condition worsens," I said. I immediately went to the limousine with Tracy to make some phone calls. Luckily for Scott and me, one of my scientist lived in the vicinity. I called him and we went to meet together at one of his labs. I was traumatized as my driver drove me to the lab; Tracy comforted me in my time of distress. I couldn't believe no healing had taken place, especially when the man was so close to dying. I felt humiliated because the healing was on live television.

I arrived at the lab and met with my friend. He quickly set up a testing procedure to determine if there was anything wrong with the stick. He said it would take at least 24 hours before he would know anything.

"Dear Lord," I said. "Scott could die by that time."

"I will do my best, David," he responded in humbleness. "Do you have any healing sticks with you?" he asked.

"No, I gave them all away to the people except a few and they are under strict lock and key with the government," I sadly replied. "It would take me a few days to get to one and I don't think we have the time."

The news in the evening was horrific. I watched in somber intensity the live clip of the hospital scene. My heart broke and I cried before the Lord. I prayed, "God, my Holy Lord, please heal Scott for he is innocent of what is going on right now, I ask you to please heal him." I quoted a Psalm of David that said, "Hear, O Lord, and answer me, for I am poor and needy. Guard my life, for I am devoted to you. You are my God; save your servant who trusts in you. Have mercy on me, O lord, for I call to you all day long" (Psalm 86:1-3).

In the morning the phone rang and it was the hospital doctor who said that Scott was near death. I quickly went to the hospital only to walk in the room when the doctor was pulling the sheet over the body of Scott. I burst into tears at the sight of seeing him being covered. Tracy made me leave and she took over the meeting with the family and hospital staff. I was in great anguish I mumbled to myself as I walked back to the limousine. "Driver, please bring me back to my hotel," I sobbed. I broke down inside my room melting into my bed like pancake batter in a hot frying pan, exhausted because the tragedy drained me of my energy.

A few hours after I passed out in utter despair, my scientist called me on the phone. "Hello," I said.

"David, I have some very bad news for you," he spoke humbly. "The stick it seems is a fake. It is not from the cross like the other sticks we have."

"I can't believe it. What could have happened to the real stick that was given to Scott?" I spurned.

"I don't know, but I think we may have some kind of bait and switch scandal here," he conceded.

"Okay," I said, "I will let Tracy and my lawyers know about it. Thank you very much for your hard work."

It didn't take long before the newspaper companies yelled, "Stop the press!" The headlines read, "David Clayton False Prophet or Not?" And other headlines read, "He healed himself, but could not heal others!" Yet others screamed, "Does David have Sin in his Life?" Isn't it funny that whenever you have a setback in your life or bad things happen to you others try to view it as you must have sin in your life? Not that something bad just happened, but that God is somehow judging you so that's why it is happening. If that were true then Peter, Paul, Stephen and John the Baptist must have lived in continual sin because all of them died terrible deaths by the hands of those who were against the gospel. Also, rather peculiar is that when you have great blessings in your life these same people now suddenly declare it is not God who blessed you it was just good luck.

I still let these things that other people say kind of bother me; however, lately I've come to realize that scoffers are just miserable people that are trying to put their misery on you. I found out that the wife and family of Scott were filing a lawsuit against me for the death of her husband. My heart went out to the family about his death. I was very saddened over the loss of such a good man. I let the family know that by paying all his funeral expenses and hospital bills they had accumulated. The lawsuit would not get them anywhere because each person who was granted a healing stick had to sign a legal waiver that included any and all possible scenarios. Still it made me feel gloomy about the whole thing for this was the first time in thousands of healings that a person was not healed when given a stick.

I was informed that there was some kind of ingenious bait and switch that went on in Scott's situation. I really don't want to talk about it too much except to say that it was disturbing that someone let an innocent man die for his or her selfish gain. These sticks could get millions of dollars if sold on the black market, so I was not at all surprised to see this happen. Nevertheless, I had to dust my feet off and try to leave what happened behind.

## PHYSICIAN HEAL THYSELF

My schedule is always so booked with all these healings and meetings and speaking engagements that I have felt like I'm constantly on the run. Tracy is like my lifesaver; she makes sure all arrangements are made for my jet and hotel rooms. Now that this tragedy of Scott has passed, I'm heading to California for a meeting with the leaders of the churches in the area. I have a nice bedroom in my jet, which helps tremendously to relieve jet lag. The pilot just informed us that we a getting ready to land in Los Angeles. I knew once we landed it would be another long drive to another city in California. It is times like these that I just pray and meditate upon the Lord. He is my comfort in the storms of life and has become to me a friend that sticks closer than a brother.

As the car pulled near our meeting place, there were the usual television crews and cameras everywhere. I got out of the car and started to walk to the crowd of people waiting when two gunshot bursts rang out from somewhere around the crowd. Instantly I was lying out on the pavement looking up into the bright blue clouds. Pain screeched through my body like I was a human cannon ball that missed its target. The blue clouds became dark, seemingly like it was going to rain. It was not rain that was making the cloud coverage dark though. It was my body passing out because of the sheer pain I was experiencing. As time dragged on I could hear the voices of people around me asking if anyone had a healing stick. I faded into oblivion again and awoke in an ambulance with sirens screaming and wailing away.

We arrived at the hospital with a team of doctors present. I was rushed into the emergency room with great swiftness. By now my pain had reached extreme levels and I was bleeding badly. I passed out again and I felt like I was experiencing life between two worlds. I could hear the doctors talking but it was all mumbled. At the same time I was fully capable of reasoning with myself intellectually. I asked God if it was His desire to bring me home. I asked Him how this could happen to me when I was doing what He called me to do.

I was bewildered over the fact that here I was, a man who had witnessed countless healings, lying on a surgical bed with doctors fluttering around me. I could hear one of the surgeons say that he was going to try to save my spine so I could walk. The first bullet plunged into my lower back and the second whizzed into my neck. I heard another doctor say that my neck would probably come out okay as far as he could tell. From my vantage point I was discussing these same things with God. Lying there while the surgeons went to work I spoke with my Heavenly Father about what the future might bring for me. I reminded God that when I was a young boy, I believed in Him even though I never had any knowledge of whom He was. I remember as a child being sprawled out on the grass looking up at the clouds as they moved. I was never sure what was going on. Were the clouds moving or was the earth moving? Never knowing the answer, it didn't matter. I was young and full of questions. I looked up into those clouds and knew God was out there somewhere. I asked God if He remembered those times we spent together.

My inner voice answered, "Yes, my child, I do remember your great faith at such a young age." I then fumbled for a way to ask God what His plans were for me now.

I could hear Him whisper to me, "You are searching for a polite way to come right out and ask me about your future, are you not, my son?"

"Yes, dear Lord, I am worried about being shot and I have always been terrified of having any type of surgery," I made my case.

God responded, "I have your life in my hands and what you're about to go through will bring glory to my name." I could hear the nurses talking about my IV's and blood pressure.

"Lord," I asked, "did you make me get shot in the back?"

"My dear child," He gently answered, "I would not do things like that to bring about my glory. For I have promised that, in all things I work for the good of those who love me, who have been called according to my purpose."

"Thank you, Lord," I answered. "Now I remember that scripture in Romans 8:28. But I can not see what good can come about with me being here having surgery, when I was supposed to be giving a speech about you?"

"I will be with you. Have faith and be comforted as you are highly esteemed before me," the Lord replied.

"Father, should I use another healing stick to heal myself once I am out of danger?" I asked.

"My dear son, take what comes upon you as your thorn in the

flesh and do not use my cross for your healing. I will in good season restore you and my glory will be complete in you," He tenderly instructed.

"I will try to the best of my ability to obey your instructions and bring glory to you, for you are my love and my Lord," I responded.

I was jostled when one of the doctors worked on my lower back. Again I faded to black while the team of surgeons operated to keep me alive. I was feeling rather groggy when I woke up many hours later. I was kind of in an eerie state of not knowing where I was. A nurse who sat by my bedside told me my mother and Tracy were outside waiting to speak to me. I told the nurse it was okay to let them in. Mom and Tracy both broke down in tears when they entered the room and saw me lying there on the bed.

"David," Mother asked gently, "how are you doing?"

"I guess I'm okay, Mom, but I don't know the extent of my injuries yet, do you?"

"The doctors will tell you when they come in. I just wanted to be with you for a few minutes before they do," she exclaimed.

The nurse asked me if it was okay for the doctors to come in now and I said yes. The head surgeon walked up to me like I was some great politician or something. He asked me if I was ready to hear about my injuries and I said I think so. He told me that my lower back had been badly damaged by the bullet wound and it was very possible I would never be able to walk again. Tears welled up in both my mom's eyes and mine as he spoke. He said I would have to go through extensive physical therapy just to be able to sit up and that it would be painful. Mother let out a little cry when he said that. I told the doctor I was willing to do all they thought I should do to get better.

Mom said, "David, get a healing stick for yourself."

"No, Mother," I replied, "what happened to me is somehow going to be turned into good. For God has promised me that I would bring Him great glory through this."

"God would get great glory by having the whole world see you getting healed by one of the sticks," she whimpered.

"Mom, if God wants to heal me without a stick, He is perfectly able to do it if it is His will," I gently replied. I then instructed the doctors to let the hospital staff know that any visitors who came to see me had to be cleared to make sure they would not use a healing stick on me. I requested that a guard be placed outside my door for this specific reason.

Mom bellowed in anger, "Oh don't be ridiculous, David. You have given away thousands of the sticks, just use one for my sake please!"

"Mother," I kindly responded, "I am here and this situation of mine has got to work itself out on its own. I cannot always be dependent on a healing stick, and besides you know that I have given them all away!"

"Come now, David. You don't expect me to believe you have no way to get your hands on even one little stick?" Mother questioned.

"Yes, Mother, I want you to believe that. I want the world to see that I am a human just as they are and I have to depend on God just as they do. Without any sticks to heal me I am as helpless as anyone," I explained.

Tracy didn't say a thing during my talk with Mom, but I could see the hurt in her face over what I was telling my mother. Our conversation ended when a nurse came in to give me some medication. I told Tracy to hire an independent security firm and a guard that would be with me wherever I went in the next few weeks so that it would be documented that I didn't have access to any healing sticks.


## JOB'S FRIENDS

I was in my physical therapy session at the hospital when one of my friends showed up to visit. Kenneth was always a cheerful, happy-go-lucky kind of guy that made me laugh. He said he had been praying for me and that the news media was having a heyday with my condition. A newspaper article title read, "David goes up against Goliath!" I had to be very careful even among family and friends because I thought they would take matters into their own hands and somehow get a stick from somewhere and poke me.

Kenneth said that radio talk shows were talking about things like what happened to Paul the Apostle. Paul was heading to Italy and the boat he was on was being tossed to and fro by violent winds of hurricane force in the sea. The storm was so intense that the men aboard were forced to throw the cargo overboard. The men were so busy securing the boat and worrying for their lives they didn't eat for fourteen days. Paul encouraged them to eat and told them they would not perish for an angel told him so. Finally the ship ran aground and they all swam ashore; no one perished as Paul had previously told them.

Once on the shore island of Malta, the islanders welcomed them with much kindness. They built a fire for them because of the cold. As Paul was gathering wood for the fire, a snake attached itself to Paul's hand. When the islanders saw the snake they said to each other, "Probably this man is a murderer, for even though he escaped from the violent storms, now he will die because justice is served and will not allow for him to live." Paul merely shook the snake off his hand and went about his business. The islanders waited for him to drop dead and when Paul didn't die then they said he must be a god. Kenneth reported some were saying I must be a god and others were saying that I suffered my due fate and became crippled because justice is served just as the islanders thought about Paul.

"That's ridiculous," I told Kenneth. "Everybody knows what happened. A fanatic shot me because he didn't like the fact that the cross was cut up and he thought I was the Antichrist. Before my bodyguards got to him he shot himself. That's all; nothing else is here for anyone to read into." I told Kenneth that I all wanted was for the world to see God work through me as a regular human being. I said that I believed that God used the healing sticks to awaken the people as His last call to us here on earth. My goal now was to let God be God in my life and I had already used my one stick for a healing.

Kenneth told me that religious people were saying that I was testing the Lord and it wasn't right because they said as the finder of the cross I should be able to use a stick, and it was embarrassing them that I was in a wheelchair for the rest of my life. I told Kenneth that I did have a lot of temptation to try and get a stick, especially when my pain was very intense. Jesus suffered the same temptation when the Bible said in Mark, "Those who passed by hurled insults at him, shaking their heads and saying, 'So! You who are going to destroy the temple and build it in three days, come down from the cross and save yourself'" (Mark 15:29,30).

"Exactly," Kenneth responded. "People are saying that you have gone insane and you think you're Jesus. They think that it's not normal for any human who could be healed not to take the healing."

"I'm not insane," I clamored, "but that kind of logic is insane!"

"Okay, David, you are my friend and I too am wondering about you. Can you give me a more logical reason for you not taking a healing stick?"

"I am trying to do what pleases God, because He assured me He would take care of me and bring glory unto Himself through this tragedy."

"Wouldn't you being healed in front of the whole world bring Him glory?" Kenneth replied.

"Maybe what happened to me is kind of like what happened to Job in the Old Testament. Remember when God was bragging about His servant Job to Satan because Job was upright and feared God?"

"Yes," Kenneth answered.

"Then Satan said that the only reason that Job was faithful to God was because he was really blessed by Him. But if you were to give me permission Satan asked to take it all away then he will curse you to your face. So in one day Job lost all his oxen, donkeys and camels as they were stolen. Then all his sheep died suddenly. Finally Job's sons and daughters were all killed and so he lost everything that was precious to him."

"If you tell this story to the public they will say that now you think you are Job," Kenneth said. "Can't you see you are fighting a losing battle with your critics?"

"Wait," I replied. "Job was still faithful to God and God bragged to Satan once again. Satan responded by telling God that if Job's life were at stake and his body ill then he would for sure curse God. So Satan struck Job with sores from his feet to his head. Even Job's wife at this time said to him, 'Why are you trying to hold out your integrity?' Job's response was, 'If we are willing to accept good from God then why not trouble?'"

"I understand this, David," Kenneth said, "but you are not in a test, you were shot in the back!"

"'Though He slay me, yet will I hope in Him' (Job 13:15). I am not saying that God did this to me, I don't believe that God would do such a thing, but I am in this condition and I am trusting the Lord to do what He sees fit in my situation," I answered.

"Oh well," Kenneth stymied, "maybe you are insane after all. I've got to go, David, I'll be praying for you, okay."

A few days later, the third person to come and try to reason with me was my cousin Justin, who was healed from cancer. "Hello, Justin," I said as he walked into my room.

"David, how are you doing?" Justin asked.

"Great, Justin, and may I say you look amazing," I replied.

"David, I came to talk with you about this madness of you trying to be crippled for the rest of your life when you know you don't have to sit in that wheelchair each and every day," Justin barked.

"Justin, I am not trying to be crippled, I am crippled," I replied.

"Yes, that's true, but you don't have to be if you don't want to be," Justin sternly said.

"I am confident that God will work this out for my good, haven't all of us seen lately that God is making Himself known to the world. That means He is in charge and I am merely putting my trust in Him, Justin!" I sounded off.

"Okay, I can see that, but what about your ministry to the world? It is being hampered by you wasting all your time here going through rehabilitation. Because you are confined to your wheelchair your true mission that you started is not being fulfilled," he clamored.

"Please try to understand, Justin. I am confidant that if I don't use a stick and trust God, He will work this out for me."

"Okay, have it your way, but remember I was once in your shoes and you came to me and told me to give you a chance and even though I didn't believe in Jesus at the time and I was full of bitterness, I still gave you permission to come to my house and try something on me that you were not even sure of yet," he spoke boldly.

"You are impressing me with how much you have matured since your healing and I will take into consideration the great things you told me today," I commented.

"Listen, I've got to run, David, so take care and do what's right. Remember that I love you no matter what you decide, okay? Take care."

With that he left me sitting all alone to ponder these three friends of Job; my mother, Kenneth, and Justin coming to me and giving me their best arguments. I have to say that I was tempted almost beyond what I could handle and Job's three friends can sound mighty wise when you are down and out.

The next morning I awakened bright and cheerful. Today I would leave the center and make my way back into the world, wheelchair and all. Even though I couldn't walk, I felt strong and healthy. Soon, I was on my jet again, with a little modification to it, and off we went into the sky blue yonder. I had to go home to take care of some things and meet with the board of Fresh Refreshment Company.

Once home my life was changed drastically because everywhere I went I was in a wheelchair now. Tracy was by my side most of the time and I enjoyed her company. My business was flourishing partly because people felt sorry for me, so they drank more soda. The miracles from the healing sticks were still coming in every day. The groups that were bent on stopping the sticks from spreading had clammed up since they realized that there was nothing in the world they could do to stop them from being given out. Revival was still spreading like wild fire and the church doors could not hold all the people. Results from other nations who got some sticks were so positive that more healings were taking place for people without the healing sticks than the tiny number of people who had them. They were just trusting God; it was an outpouring of God's grace on all inhabitants of the world. I was enriched by what I was seeing and even though my own situation was a bit off kilter, God's plan was in full bloom. I was inspired by all the happenings around the globe.

# WHAT I'VE LEARNED

My personal life was still under attack, for the enemies of the cross were always trying to make me look bad. When speaking to a small group at a church, I talked about this. My comments were pretty down to earth as I said to the group, "These critics of mine have been trying to dig up anything they can about my past to see if I was really holy. They still do not get it that I have always said that I am not some kind of saint. I have had sins in the past that maybe some still hold against me. That was long ago and minor in comparison to the world. In the Book of Psalms it says, 'As far as the east is from the west, so far has he removed our transgressions from us' (Psalm 103:12). Let's analyze this for a moment, when does the east ever meet the west?" I asked. "Never, right? So can you see that our sins are behind the back of God. 'For I will forgive their wickedness and will remember their sins no more' (Jeremiah 31:34). And again the Bible says, 'Because by one sacrifice he has made perfect forever those who are being made holy' (Hebrews 10:14). Please see that it says He had made us perfect forever.

"God says, 'Never will I leave you; never will I forsake you' (Hebrews 13:5). Now there are those among us who want to keep dragging us down over the sins of the past. These people are acting as your judges. It is the bitterness in their hearts that won't allow them to let go of the past and press on to the future. But they will say to me that you, David, are living in constant sin, you deliberately sin, and in fact you destroyed the authentic cross of Jesus. You have to live with the guilt of what you have done every day. Really: who doesn't deliberately sin, who hasn't done wrong in their lives? Jesus said, 'Therefore I tell you, do not worry about your life, what you will eat or drink; or about your body, what you will wear. Is not life more important than food, and the body more important than clothes' (Matthew 6:25). Is not worrying a sin just as the others? Is not trusting God for the things in your life by worrying actually telling Him you don't believe He can take care of you? In fact, worrying is like a slap in God's face and to Him it is actually one of the worst things you can do in His eyes. It is interesting to note that right after talking about worrying the Bible goes straight to this, 'Do not judge, or you too will be judged. For in the same way you judge others, you will be judged' (Matthew 7:1). This is not talking about when somebody has done severe crimes or whatever against you and we cannot come against them. You have to take it, as it is meant, not out of context and say we are not allowed to come against anybody no matter what they do. Christians aren't holy doormats!

"But those who come against you will use scriptures that they have no clue as to what their meaning is. For instance, 'It is impossible for those who have once been enlightened…' (Hebrews 6:4). And, 'If we deliberately keep on sinning after we have received the knowledge of the truth…' (Hebrews 10:26). I know them all and I also understand what they mean. As a Christian you need to understand what these scriptures are talking about or other people will bind you up with their hateful interpretations to put you down! Most often the people in your life who attack and accuse you of living in sin spend the least amount of time studying the Word of God! That is why they come against you with scriptures they know nothing about.

"You need to know that some people are downright mad when you have discovered, 'It is for freedom that Christ has set us free' (Galatians 5:1). They hate the fact that you have gone on with your life and are full of happiness and joy. These people want you to live within the confines of their bitterness towards you. They will lock you up if you let them, but I encourage each of you to be strong in the Lord.

"Finally, 'Blessed is the man whose sin the Lord will never count against him' (Romans 4:8). If God Himself can forgive our sin, what right does any other person have to put you down? Take heart, church, and grow in the grace of God, for it is only by grace you have been saved. Please remember that, 'It does not, therefore depend on man's desire or effort, but on God's mercy' (Romans 9:16). I hope you have enjoyed our study together and may your journey with Christ be filled with the pure love and excitement that I have found in being a child of God."

I opened up for questions. One young woman asked me why it was that I always talk about my love for God. I replied, "God made mankind for companionship and He gave us our free will because He didn't want robotic love. He wanted us to love Him on our own. When a person truly seeks God and understands His Word, then the heart cannot help but fall in love knowing what God has done. I can honestly say that I am madly in love with God and my heart is filled with the joy He gives. This didn't come easy. I sought the Lord and learned His personality and then our relationship blossomed into a beautiful love story. Many Christian people think they will find this by just going to church a couple times a week, but even though my schedule doesn't always allow me to be in church, I have a twenty-four hour ongoing relationship with the Lord. That is how my love grows daily in the midst of worldly problems."

With that, I answered a few more personal questions for the group, but most were interested in the healings that came about from the cross. In my situation I am constantly monitored for what I say and do, this is why I used this opportunity of speaking to the church group concerning the gossip that some wanted to spread about me. I know that whatever I say will get back to those who wish to see me fail. I know they will read the transcripts because they are curious over the events in my life.

Some of the critics that dragged my name down over my decisions concerning the cross were like thirsty bloodhounds hot on my trail. Articles came up about how could God choose such a person as myself to be the one to find the cross. They stated I wasn't suited to be the so-called leader of this great revival that was literally sweeping the whole world. Great men of God abounded throughout the world, but who was I? It reminded me when certain men, upon seeing the great miracles of Paul, tried to cast out evil spirits as Paul did and so these men went to a demon-possessed man and tried to cast the demons out. The demon-possessed man spoke sternly to those who really had no power and said, "Jesus I know, and I know about Paul, but who are you?" (Acts 19:15). Then the man gave them such a beating they ran out of the house naked and bleeding (Acts 19:16). The snares of the devil easily beat people who know Jesus by name only, and have never taken the time to know Him personally. It doesn't matter if you go to church; notice the demons didn't ask whether they attended church or not, they just knew what spirit was living inside of them.

The ironic thing about this big controversy is that I am not the leader of this great world revival, God is. I am just a person who loved archeology and desired to find the cross of Jesus Christ. Never in a million years did I think this kind of outpouring of the Holy Spirit would come upon the planet as a result of finding the greatest historical piece of all time. I did not ask to be chosen for this task; it was given to me just the same way David was chosen by Samuel. God told Samuel, go to the house of Jesse and I will show you who is to be the next king. First Samuel met Eliab and thought for sure this was God's anointed for he was tall and strong. The Lord said to Samuel that He does not look upon outward appearance, but looks to the heart. Then Abinadab came before Samuel, but he was not chosen either. Then Shammah came, but he was not chosen. Eventually Jesse had seven of his sons stand before Samuel and Samuel said, "The Lord has not chosen these." So he asked Jesse, "Are these all the sons you have?" (1 Samuel 16:10,11). Jesse replied that there was still the youngest son, but he was busy tending the sheep out in the fields. So Samuel asked for Jesse to send for him. When David appeared before Samuel, the Bible says David was ruddy, he had a fine appearance about him and he was handsome. The Lord told Samuel rise up and anoint him because he was the one whom He chose. After Samuel anointed David that day the Spirit of the Lord came upon David in power.

Now I am not saying that I am ruddy, handsome and have a fine appearance. God chose David because of his heart, not because he was strong and wise. So if there is any reason for God choosing me to be the finder of the cross it is only because I have a heart of love for God. "God chose the foolish things of the world to shame the wise; God chose the weak things of the world to shame the strong." (1 Corinthians 1:27). My weakness has been shown to the whole world, my life has become an open book for all to read. The more I am in the midst of this great outpouring, the weaker I become. I have no desire for any praise or glory; my only hope is that the world will see that God loves them and is calling them unto Himself. When I was in Israel I wrote this down one thundering stormy night. I called it, "The rains descended, the love came."

*The heavens declare the power of God while the earth rocks to and fro. His might is seen by everyone as lightening stretches its glow. The voice of God speaks loudly as thunder roars His command; get ready my people I'm coming soon to take you to another land.*

*In the midst of this confusion His love is clearly seen, with gentleness a still strong voice whispers very keen. I love you and died for you, I carried my cross you know and with your sin they nailed it in as blood ran out my bones. My heart was crying, my body was dying, my God where are you now? Forsaken, alone, but no broken bones for you my life was given. If you'll only receive and just believe I'll sup with you in heaven.*

# CHAPTER 7
# Your Eyes are Doves

My life has drastically changed since I've been confined to a wheelchair. The ease of just getting up and doing whatever I want has now been tried with much difficulty. Before, I never really thought about how much just being able to walk makes your life a lot easier. When things are taken from you is always when you miss them the most and I had been experiencing this firsthand for the first time in my life. Instead of just bouncing up the stairs of my jet, now I had to be lifted and the whole ordeal did make me feel somewhat sad in knowing that in one split second, in the blink of an eye, I could plunge a stick into my body and this trial would be all over with. Maybe I was starting to give in to the constant hounding of Job's friends. Their words rang in my ears constantly, especially when having to depend on someone else to help me. I certainly have come to gain an immense amount of respect for all those people who have had to live in wheelchairs and with disabilities as a whole. My burden would be lessened when I thought of the time when I would be running in heaven, free as a dove fluttering in the crisp clean air.

My most appreciated person in my life was Tracy. She had been with Fresh Refreshment Company for around twelve years now and she started working for us at a young age just out of college. I have known Tracy since kindergarten; we were childhood friends and buddies. I remember when I was about seven years old we had a German Shepard named Lucky. I called for him to come back because when he got out of the yard he went running down the street in a mad dash to gain his freedom. Lucky turned around and came running back towards me. He looked like a freight train coming at me and I tried to climb one of those steel street light posts, but it was too slippery. I kind of slid onto the sidewalk when Lucky hit me like I was rag doll. I went sailing into the air and skidded on the blacktop street. I was hurt very bad and I was flattened out looking up. Suddenly there was Tracy standing above me; she told me to lie still and she would get my mom. I never forgot that gentle voice at a time when I thought I was dying. Mother came out to pick me up and my back was scraped so bad I lost the top layer of skin. In spite of my pain there was Tracy. It seems like whenever I get hurt she is somehow with me. Maybe she's my guardian angel?

Our families were very good friends together as well. She knew my father like her own and she was devastated when he passed away. On and off throughout high school we went out together, but not as boyfriend and girlfriend. She usually was my assistant when I was at work in the office, or if I had business meetings she would go with me and take care of the important issues surrounding our meetings. Mom would always say to me, right in front of her, "David, doesn't Tracy look absolutely beautiful today?"

"Yes, Mom," I would answer. We have spent countless hours together working and even on trips to other cities and such, so we ate out many times in restaurants and outings just trying to survive business issues around the country. It's funny in all this time I never really looked at Tracy as a woman. Of course I noticed her when she dressed up very pretty, because she is an extremely beautiful woman. I mean, I didn't look at her in the way of being attracted to her like a dating relationship. Most likely it is because when I am working it is all just business for me.

But ever since I have been disabled after the gunshot wounds, Tracy has been with me constantly. Whatever I need she's there, whatever I want she gets for me. I have always paid her way over the average wage for her dedication to her job and me personally as her boss. I have been overly generous in bonuses for her on out-of-state business dealings she went on with me. When I went to Israel, sometimes I felt like a fish out of water because Tracy was not there with me on the archeology trip. I have never taken her for granted. I wonder now more then ever what in the world I would do without her. She was with me the day I was shot and rode in the ambulance alongside of me holding my hand in hers, which was what gave me comfort. She gently stroked my hand during the drive and spoke words of encouragement all the way to the hospital. "David, can you hear me," she whispered. "I am here with you and you are going to be just fine. I will be by your side and pray for you."

Tracy was really a strong Christian who loved God with all her heart. She comes from a fantastic family who all were strong believers. The positiveness that flowed from her father and mother was enough to make a person think they could accomplish anything in life. Her brothers and sisters were just great down-to-earth human beings. I loved being around them because I could feel like a kind of a silent buzzing energy that radiated off them like sun rays on your body on a hot day at the beach. Of course, because I wasn't seeking God during those days, I never truly realized that it was God in their lives that gave them this glow of joyful living. I needed her now more than ever and I was totally obligated to her for traveling from city to city and wheeling me around.

We had just gotten inside my jet and Tracy was wheeling me close to my seat before take off. I was not only physically exhausted, I was mentally exhausted also. I had been pushing the limit trying to prove to everybody that my disability wouldn't slow me down. I was putting up a good front to the world, but Tracy saw it in my actions that I was physically drained.

After I was all strapped in, the jet readied for take off. I hate taking off and landing because it always puts my body in such a tense state that I think if I fell I would just crack in two like a cement statue. Tracy's area was in front with the other workers who would go along when they were needed. Once in the air I hoped that I would be able to get some rest, even though for me on a plane it is nearly impossible. But pure and ragged exhaustion won me over. Soon I was sleeping soundly and it felt great. I must have slept for three hours without even moving a peep. I had sugarplums dancing in my head. The sheep didn't dare show up to bother me I was in such a deep sleep.

# AN ANGEL OF THE LORD

I began to have a vision, I wasn't sure if it was an angel or not. But this beautiful creature was coming towards me with locks of hair that shined a glow that pierced into my being like a dagger. The most beautiful eyes I've ever seen galloped out to me like a Clydesdale horse that just won first prize for overall beauty. A face that was the most structurally sound light beam in the entire world. Each line was perfectly in place; each tone was pitched in perfect harmony. Like a symphony in an extravagant play this face chained me up as a prisoner in my own body. I heard what was a question flowing in my soul like I was standing under a waterfall drinking in the purest, cleanest water that was drenching me entirely. The tender words seemed to be saying something to this effect, "What I have given you, as a gift to show you my love, accept and do not turn away that which is from above!"

Suddenly I was coming out of this immaculate trance-like condition and I heard the voice of an angel. "David, David, your choice is ready and it is exquisite." My eyes began to slowly glide open and I saw the angel speaking to me and I beheld all her glory. It was Tracy, standing there with my choice prime rib. Her hair was down and she had not had it cut it for a few years now. Usually, she wore it up where it wasn't so overpowering, but there she stood with all her glory right before me. I was dazed to see her looking so divine; my heart was beating wildly as she beckoned my complete being like a princess in a fairy tale. She set my dinner down in front of me and I feebly asked her if she would come sit next to me to enjoy our dinner together.

Once we were all situated and ready to eat, I asked her if she was just walking towards me a few minutes ago, before I awoke.

She said, "Yes, I was, but you seemed to be in a trance-like state."

"I was having a vision of an angel coming towards me and I heard the voice of God speak to me," I reported.

"That's funny," she gently responded, "because as I was walking towards you your eyes were partially open."

Suddenly, I came to understand the vision of beauty I beheld in such great devotion was Tracy and God was telling me that His gift was here and for me not to turn her away. I wondered if somehow she knew that I was in complete rapture over her beauty as she came towards me. So I kind of fumbled a statement. "Tracy, I have never seen your hair down like this, it's very beautiful!"

"Thank you, David," she replied. "I just had a perm done and I wanted it to relax so I let my hair down."

Suddenly, for the first time in all the years we spent together, after all the dinners, all the flights, all the business meetings I felt like I didn't know what to say. It was kind of like when you first meet a gorgeous woman and you are star struck and then you are tongue-tied. I really had myself in a pickle like a seventh grader who was being asked to dance for the first time by the prettiest girl in school.

"Are you okay, David?" she questioned.

I was in really big trouble by now, and I pointed to my throat to signify that I couldn't speak yet. I had to buy a minute or two to think of what to say. Talk about sticky situations! I prayed, "Lord, you got me into this with your vision and telling me to accept this gift, please untie my tongue or this is going to be very humiliating." As I mumbled out some inaudible words, I felt like I was the most vulnerable man on the planet Earth, except I wasn't on the planet, I was in a plane floating in heavenly fluffy clouds.

"When we land and rest for a day would you like to come over to my parents' house Saturday for their fortieth wedding anniversary?" she asked.

"I love you," I replied. "I mean I'd love to," I stammered.

She kind of giggled like second grade girls do when you're handing them a valentine. "Don't forget that next week you are scheduled to take another MRI to see how your back is doing and I will be picking you up at nine in the morning on Thursday also,"

Tracy said quietly.

"Next week already, how time flies when you're swept off your feet. I mean, when you're stuck in a seat. You know my wheelchair," I fumbled like a quarterback who threw the ball with butter in his hands.

"Are you sure you're okay? You're acting kind of strange," she persevered.

"Must be the pain pills I took before we lifted off," I cautioned. "Anyways, I would really like to see your parents again. I haven't see them in a while," I conceded.

"You know they love you very much and last time I talked to my mother she told me she had the whole church praying for you and hoping for your best," she chimed.

"Thanks, Tracy, you always know how to make me feel better. You know we have been the closest friends for so many years and I was wondering how come we never went out on a date together? I don't mean a business dinner or outing, I mean a date, do you know what I mean?" I asked clumsily.

"Because you never asked me out!" she replied.

"Ouch, that's true, okay let me rephrase the question. I was wondering why would a man who has known a wonderful women for his whole life, that is totally beautiful, honest, caring and has eyes that shine like diamonds and not ever think to ask her out?" She giggled like Wilma Flintstone and I felt like Barnie Rubble.

"Now that's more like it," she coined. "I haven't been able to figure it out myself either, after all we get along like best friends," she said.

"You know, Tracy, I have to be honest with you, my life has been like a whirlpool. Let me look up that word in my computer. Whirlpool: Whirling mass of water having a depression in the center. That pretty much fits, doesn't it?" I agreed. The cook came to take our plates away, as we had just finished eating.

"That seems to fit the bill pretty much, but I don't think you missed the boat yet, there's still hope for you," she quipped.

"Do you know that when we were in grade school I was in love with you?" I stuttered.

"I didn't know that because I was in love with you too!" she quietly answered. "How come you never let me know how you felt?"

"Because I thought you were too pretty to fall for someone like me," I quivered.

"We have a lot of catching up to do as far as hiding our feelings all these years and I hope that we can try to see if this is what God wants for us both," Tracy said lovingly. "Okay, Dave, we should rest our eyes a little before we land."

"Of course, you rest and have sweet dreams. I hope my dreams have come true today," I answered.

She grasped my hand playfully and we both closed our eyes to rest. My heart was in state of Disneylandish euphoria. If there is such a word. After so many times we spent together I suddenly had something come over me that was so overwhelming it took the very life out of me, filled me up again and I was thrown back into myself, or should I say slammed back into myself? *What on earth just took place?* I was thinking. My vision was Tracy in all her splendor. I had an epiphany and it was miraculous. I hadn't felt this many butterflies since I first stuck my finger with a healing stick. Now, I was worried about seeing Tracy's parents. I wondered if they would notice that something within me had changed when I gazed at her. I hoped I wouldn't end up acting like it was a high school prom and I was asking them for permission to take their daughter as my date.

Delicately Tracy's head gently cradled onto my shoulder and I thought the world was turning from ashes to beauty. I could smell the perfume she sprayed to cover up the perm and with her long flowing hair spilling over to my seat I, for the first time in my life, felt like it was all coming together. I was emancipated and my heart broke loose like a hundred helium air balloons seeking their freedom. My ears heard church bells ringing, ringing as if they were calling, calling me home. A satisfaction always comes over me when I hear church bells clanging and my heart just seems to fall in love when there's something so real. Something that is beyond life and inside you, then you realize you have found home.

*Dear Lord, I prayed silently. How could I have gone for so long and never felt the feelings that I have felt in just the last few hours? What inside me held me from totally letting go of myself and giving my heart to somebody else so completely? Was it all in timing or was it a woman who just spilled such kindness completely unto me over my whole lifetime that broke the eggshell of my heart? Lord, I may never know how your great plan falls into our laps at times, yet I am so thankful to you that you have given me this chance to love in my life when it seemed love wasn't a gift I would ever find. I am forever in your gratitude. I promise to always keep my heart madly in love with you, my Redeemer. May my soul lift you up forever without end, Amen.*

I felt words welling up inside me like a spring of living water as Tracy's hair composed my soul with our heads touching so close together.

"Cherry cola, a cool summer breeze, a walk by the ocean, hearing a baby sneeze. Seagulls flying up above, white clouds up in the sky, burying my feet in the sand, a child's lullaby. Grassy hillsides, a beautiful butterfly, silence in the night, rainbows in the sky.

"Swimming in clear water, walking by moonlight, opening up my heart to you, being by my side. These things I enjoy like a soft touch of your hand, memories and pleasant thoughts of a promised land.

"Life brings many heartaches, love's a lock and chain, the key lies within us, open it for a change."

I was in a spirit of oneness with my God. His plan was in full swing and as with everything else, right on time. If a relationship with Tracy did blossom, I wondered if I should get ahold of a healing stick to make it easier. Would God, who told me to trust in Him, be betrayed if I were to go the easy route and claim healing with a stick? As Tracy's hair was spilling onto my lap, I wondered if this was similar to the story of Sampson and Delilah. Where Sampson had long beautiful locks of hair, which was his strength, and in weakness he told Delilah his secret and she had his hair cut off which resulted in him losing all his strength. Could Tracy's long beautiful locks have been the trigger that after all these years sent my heart reeling so quickly? Is this temptation for me to take a stick and lose my reward as God told me to trust in Him? I was filled with many ifs, coulds, and wonders. But though it may have been me seeing her in a semi-state of sleep walking towards me that released these desires that I had kept hidden for her for so long, what about the voice, the voice that spoke to me and told me to accept this gift?

*Oh well,* I concluded, *it's in God's hands now and if what happened here on a leer jet is real, then it will continue when both our feet are firmly planted on the ground. I can only do what I have always done and that is give it to God and let Him take control. If I can leave a billion dollar soft drink company for others to run and trust them, then why can't I trust God for something as simple as love between a man and a woman?*

Our pilot came over the speaker and told us to buckle up, we were getting ready to land soon. I felt like I never wanted to land, my heart was soaring like our plane and I didn't want it to end. Tracy started to wake up and she realized the she was practically in my seat with me.

"Oh, I'm terribly sorry. I must have really been knocked out," she whispered.

"Tracy, you can always lean on me anytime you want," I responded.

## TESTED BY FIRE

When the plane touched down and we were on solid ground, we were met by one of my good friends who went with me to Israel to find the cross

"David, Tracy," he spoke sternly, "I'm afraid I have some terrible news to tell you both. We have had another healing stick switch scandal and there is a young boy who is in serious trouble," he exclaimed.

"Oh no not again," I reacted with regret.

"A little before we had the lottery for the sticks he was chosen to receive one because he was badly burned in a house fire that left him with burns all over his body. Both his parents died from smoke inhalation, but little Michael escaped with his life. The sad news is that before he crawled out of the house he was burned so bad he was in critical condition," he declared.

"Dear Jesus please help him," Tracy said sorrowfully.

"David," my friend said, "he needs a stick very soon."

"I will try to do what I can as fast as possible," I said to him. "Tracy, can you call our lab director and explain to him our situation? I would hate to have another healing stick fiasco, especially with a young innocent child," I agonized.

"I will get right to it," she replied.

We left together in the limousine and I went home and Tracy went to her house. She only lived a few miles from me, which made it convenient for us. About four hours later Tracy called and said she had gotten a stick and they wanted us to meet them at the burn unit in the hospital. My limo driver wheeled me out and we went to pick up Tracy and we met our lab director there. The sticks are almost impossible to come up with nowadays because for the most part they have been given away. I did make an arrangement with the American government to keep some aside and I did have access to some in extremely special circumstances and that's how we were able to get a stick.

We met the boy's doctor and discussed his condition. The doctor said he was in very bad shape and hoped this would be the end of the young boy's suffering. When we entered the burn unit, he was sleeping, so we decided to stick him while he was asleep. I asked Tracy to be the one to do it and she kind of squirmed over the thought. But her heart was so broken that tears welled up in her eyes and she said, "My dear Lord, please heal this child in Jesus's name."

I sat by Tracy's side when she poked the stick into the boy. He quickly squealed and turned over holding his arm where the stick penetrated his skin. He looked up at both Tracy and I and said, "Mom, Dad, have you come to take me home?" I instantly glanced at Tracy and our eyes met, like energy beams coming together that could split atoms, we became one. Tracy then turned her attention to the boy and patted his head.

She instinctively spoke kind, gentle words to the young boy. She said, "Michael, when you are ready and strong it will be time for you to go home."

"I feel ready now, I don't have any pain anymore," his little voice shivered.

The doctor gently pulled the sheet off the boy and his skin was back to its original color. There was no scars form the devastation of that horrible fire. I thought he was going to faint as he said, "Today I have seen a miracle that I've never witnessed before in all my years of medical work. I will never doubt the healing power of God."

"Doctor, it is amazing and remarkable what we've seen here and witnessed," I spoke strongly. Tracy handed the boy a stuffed animal clown that kind of looked like Ronald McDonald. I was surprised because as a child that was my favorite toy. I wondered if maybe when we were kids if Tracy ever knew that was my favorite. I never told her, but she did used to play in my room when we were children and she saw it all the time. I wondered if she bought it to have some kind of closeness to me. She told Michael that it was her own clown and she wanted him to have it. My heart melted like an ice cream cone in the summertime.

The doctor had the nurse take care of Michael because they wanted to check him completely. I don't think he even knew he was no longer burned he was too young to understand, but he did know that he wasn't in the pain as he was in before. This miracle was not broadcast all over the nation because the hospital didn't want a convergence upsetting the boy. Our hearts burned within us, and Tracy and I knew when we looked into each other's eyes, we both felt love for Michael. After a brief talk with doctors we went home, and Tracy told me not to forget about Saturday at her parents.

Strange things were going on in different parts of the world that were without explanation. In Haiti, for example, they were given some healing sticks. Because they were given such a small number of the sticks, the government issued regular toothpicks to every man, women and child in their country. The people who got the real sticks were not told about it and the people who got regular toothpicks were not told they were plain ordinary toothpicks. Something wonderful was going on in their country. I was completely astonished when I watched the live televised reports coming directly from Haiti. People were getting healed all over the place and I think I was told they were only given twelve real healing sticks. The people didn't know that and some that were blind received their sight again. Crippled people were walking again and deaf people heard again. The scene was so incomprehensible that it looked liked a huge church service where an evangelist comes and people are getting healed. I could not put into words how great joy flooded my being while sitting in my wheelchair watching the wonderful commotion. It was heaven on earth in Haiti and they deserved it because for so long they had been broken with no hope of anything in their lives. The government there issued a decree making a national healing sticks week that would become part of their country's law from then on.

My night was pleasant and it felt good to be home again. I felt safe at home because after I was shot at I built a fence around the property; from inside my yard it looked like I had a moat around the house. A builder came and did some things that he said made my house impossible to break into and my yard also. Mother called and we talked awhile. I think she heard something in my voice because when I talked about going to the hospital with Tracy she said she was hoping we would keep seeing each other more outside of work. "Mom," I exclaimed, "maybe your prayers are coming true!"

I had a meeting with my company's board in the morning and I longed within myself to see Tracy's beautiful face. It was more difficult for me just to get in bed and I had some modifications done on my house to help get around better with a wheelchair. As I rested in my bed, I thought about King David when he was in Jerusalem. It was springtime and David had sent his armies off to war against the Ammonites. One cool evening David was walking around on the rooftop of his palace. His eyes suddenly saw one of the most beautiful women ever, and she was bathing. It wasn't like he was a peeping Tom or anything because Bath Sheba was in the courtyards that were a part of her house. Because David's palace was so much higher, he could look down and see the city. The lamplight caught his eye and there she was bathing herself. He was totally taken by her beauty and inquired whom she was. She was brought to him and the rest is history. In the same way I was taken aback when I glanced at Tracy coming down the jet's aisle that fateful day. I could only hope that I was in God's will concerning Tracy just like in spite of King David's sin God still called him a man after his own heart. My night's sleep was pleasant.

The next day at work we had our business meeting as usual and then the board wanted to throw an idea at me they were working on. They wanted to have a campaign to increase sales of our soda line. They told me the idea was to have one can out of the next year's whole supply have a special thing in it that if you were the lucky one you would win a healing stick. They said that sales would go through the roof and thought it was a marketing genius. What they didn't expect was that when I heard the idea I almost went through the roof. I told them that the healing sticks were given to people that were desperate and in life and death situations and I would never give false hope to anyone just to make money. I was so irate I felt like Jesus when he cleared out the moneychangers in the church. But instead of coming unglued, I explained it to them in a civil manner. I told them that I appreciated them coming up with certain advertisement campaigns to get us where we were today, but this was too personal and we were talking about people's lives. That was why the sticks were given away free in a lottery-style manner. I could have been the richest man on the planet Earth, but it wouldn't be right to buy and sell Gods healings. I explained that just as Jesus gave His life freely for us, we gave the sticks freely for the people. I got a standing ovation and I told my board that is why they were so successful, because they were able to take certain things and bounce right back.

After the meeting I wheeled into Tracy's office and asked her if she wanted to go out to lunch with me. I cupped my hand over my mouth and whispered, "This is not a business lunch either!"

Tracy cupped her hand over her mouth and whispered back,

"Okay, I accept the invitation, but only if you order my lunch for me."

"I didn't know you were such a romantic, " I questioned.

"I think you do know that," she responded.

Our lunch was great; we sat outside in a patio-style restaurant and started talking about the good old days. "Tracy," I said suddenly, "do you remember the red berries?" The red berries, as we called it, was when we were all in about third grade. We were bored one day after school and so a group of us kids went over to play in the school grounds. As we were playing some kind of hide-n-seek game, we saw a janitor cleaning up one of the classrooms. Somebody got the idea to pick the red berries off the bushes and run into the classroom and throw them inside where the janitor was sweeping. So we all picked a handful and off we went to accomplish our mission. We sneaked into the classroom and at the same time we all jumped up and screamed out as loud as we could and threw the berries into the classroom. We ran as fast as we could and jumped into some bushes to hide ourselves. The janitor was beside himself, hunting for us like a man wanting to kill wild game.

We decided to do it again, but make it scarier this time. We got a rope and with about four feet between each of us we tied ourselves all together. There must have been about six or seven of us all tied up. We figured this would make it more exciting. We went back to the school and picked our handful of red berries and scurried to the same classroom with the same janitor sweeping up the mess we just made. Again we ran into the room screaming like wild wolves and threw the berries. The janitor went berserk and as we ran away he saw that we were all tied together. We actually had half us run one way around a brick beam and the other half the other way. We had to untangle ourselves with the janitor gaining on us. He yelled at us that he had us now. My heart was beating out of my body in fear, but we got a good lead ahead of him because we were young and could run fast. When he saw he was losing us, he picked up a big rock and threw it at us. The rock hit the edge of the brick wall just as I was turning the corner. I was almost beaned in the head with a rock just for doing what we thought was normal for children.

Tracy almost cried from laughing and remembering that fateful day. "I was so scared," she said. "I had never done such a crazy thing like that before. My mother would have grounded me for life if we got caught. David, we were insane, don't you think?"

"Still are today, I guess. After all, look how many years I wasted with you and never told you how I felt," I graveled.

She reached over and touched my hand and said, "We're still only in our early thirties and still have a whole life ahead with each other if we want."

"I want," I replied. Here we were on the ground, not twenty thousand feet in the air like before, and the romance that started in the clouds was still in the clouds. Each moment with her was exhilarating; this love I had was not just formed, it had been in my heart since I was a child. So I asked her how she felt about me. Tracy was the kind of person I could say or ask anything to and she wouldn't be upset.

"You've been given many signs by me forever," she said. "I've been madly in love with you since the first day you moved next door to me. You had me at, 'Ooh, Dad, a girl moved in next door!'"

We both laughed hysterically and it was hard not to want to kiss her right there in front of everybody. We drove in Tracy's car, which made it rough because she had to put my wheelchair in the trunk. It wasn't that heavy though because it was an expensive one made out of lightweight material.

## SIGNS IN THE SKY

Driving back to work, we saw something in the sky that was unexplainable. Tracy pulled off the road and we looked on to see what looked like a meteor streaking across the sky. We both were in an amazed and frightened condition. There had never been anything so close and huge as this right in front of our eyes. It was an absolute perplexing thing to see.

Later on when I was home again the news reported that it was a meteor that traveled around the globe and the whole world saw it. We were definitely in the last days and signs were showing in the sky. A few days later in China it was reported that in broad daylight it suddenly became dark for about a minute or two. Newscasts showed the footage and it was astonishing. The churches went on red alert. Pastors were getting their congregations in order, readying them for the Rapture of the Church. Still as before, baseball stadiums were being filled, as the churches couldn't hold the number of people coming. The Bible says God would pour out His Spirit on all flesh and He was. We were watching it firsthand. Bible prophesy was coming alive right before our eyes. Newspapers had special sections in them just to report on Bible prophesy. The web sites that spoke about prophecy were flooded with people seeking the truth. Some of the web sites crashed by overload. The world was moving at an incredible rate of speed it seemed, but inside of me I felt a supernatural peace.

I prayed and asked God if He was upset that I was so madly in love with Tracy. I told God that if it seemed I love her too much then I would try to calm it down. I consulted with a Christian man who knew the word of the God forward and backwards. He let me know that God was pleased that a man should have such love for a woman; in fact he said it was representative of Christ and His church! Now I understood a little better why Adam yelled out with excitement when he saw Eve and said, "Wow!" It wasn't just her beauty; it was because he knew that God had given him a wonderful gift.

Saturday came and I had my limousine pick Tracy up for her parents' anniversary. I thought it would be a nice gesture to take them in a ride for their anniversary. Tracy's parents were very pleased that we were dating. Even though it had been for only a short time, it seemed natural because we had been together most of our lives. I told her parents that it must be wonderful to be with the same person for forty years. They said it wasn't always easy, but with kindness and understanding it could work. I looked at Tracy's mother and saw this warm-hearted, easygoing personality and I thanked her because Tracy was the same way.

I have always believed that when a man first meets a woman he wants companionship. But after marriage he mostly wants a wife who allows him to live in peace and quiet. Love and companionship are still needed, but when a man is frustrated and has to walk on pins and needles in his own home then he can never be content. Of course the same is true for a woman and what she wants from her husband. Who wants to go through life fighting and arguing every day? I'll never forget a comic strip I saw once where a soldier was in a foxhole with bombs exploding all around him and was writing a letter to his wife that said, "Please, honey, don't write me any more letters. Let me fight this war in peace!" If a good man is given the opportunity to live with a kind-hearted women who is trusting, understanding and peaceful, I hope that man will be a good husband. I have seen many marriages where there is constant friction and it just wears a couple's love out.

It was so romantic to see Tracy's parents exchange their wedding vows again after forty years. We held hands as they recited their vows. Tracy was squeezing my hand to confirm that she loved me too. That was our secret message of saying I love you without words. The celebration was in their backyard, which was huge and decorated like a wedding that was happening for the first time. Afterwards we had a very nice dinner and Tracy asked me to go for a walk. Hand in hand we strolled with me in an electric scooter to a nearby tree that had a tree house built in it. A wooden swing was hanging from the branches of the tree so we sat and swung back and forth silently.

My spirit was in flames of passion and my mind was sound. A bird chirped a love song for us as I looked longingly into Tracy's beautiful blue eyes and I asked her if she would ever consider marrying a man in a wheelchair.

"Tracy," I said, "have you ever thought about that?"

"David," she responded, "I would only marry a man for his heart and nothing else. It has nothing to do with outward appearance, money or anything else. The fact that you're in a wheelchair is not an issue, because I've loved you since childhood and still do," she exclaimed.

"Please give me few minutes to say what's in my heart. You know my heart is racing right now because I want to ask you if you would be willing to let me love you with all my vigor, with all my soul and spend the rest of your life with me forever, together as my wife," I pleaded. "You don't have to answer me now because I would rather that you think about our love and a commitment that will last our whole lives. I can promise you this, I will always be kind and understanding to your feelings. I will never treat you as though you do not mean the world to me even when are around people at work, friends or family. The way I try to show you my respect now is the way I will show you respect forty years from now. I will treat you with the gentleness just as Jesus treats each of us. If you become my wife, you will become my heart that is one with God forever," I sputtered.

"I don't need to think it over, David," she gently said. "I have been believing by faith that this day would come and with everything within me, I say yes to you!"

We fell in each other's arms and kissed. I was having my dreams come true and it was because I had been faithful to God and He was giving me the desires of my heart. After we sat for a while, we went back to the celebration and announced our own wedding.

# THE CHILD WITHIN

After the reception was over, Tracy and I headed home. I sent the limo back to let Tracy's parents go on a pleasant drive. Thursday morning I had my MRI taken again, because I wanted to see why my lower back was feeling funny. The tests came in a few weeks later and my doctor showed me the comparison of the previous MRI.

"David," he said, "your body seems to be getting better every time I see you. Do you feel like you're stronger?"

"In certain ways yes, but at other times no," I reported.

"I think that if your back and neck keep improving at this rate it is very possible that you could be walking again in about six months, maybe a little longer. My observation is that ultimately you will be perfect, as normal as you were before!" he claimed.

"Doctor, you know that the world is anxiously waiting to see if I keep my word about waiting for God's healing without using a stick. I have to have these MRI's on public display so my healing, when it comes, will bring glory to God." I exclaimed.

"I'll have them ready for you whenever you ask. I still want you to be careful and not lift anything that will reverse this trend, okay?" the doctor instructed.

"You got it, doctor, and thank you for everything," I replied.

Tracy was ecstatic over the news and our wedding was only a few days away. We didn't want some great big huge wedding. We just wanted our families and a few friends to witness our commitment.

The world scene was still reeling with tremendous excitement over the sticks. I watched on television with absolute amazement what was going on in Indonesia. They had two young boys about six years old that were Siamese twins. The boys were joined together at the head. The country wanted to use the healing sticks they got in a surgery that involved separating them. The boys were flown to a more modern hospital in another country to do the surgery. Doctors were chosen from other countries to be involved because of the risk. Their plan was to separate the boys as quickly as possible and then to poke them each with a healing stick to see what would happen. They had the surgery set up so that after separation the boys would be operated on individually to contain conditions that could bring death. The overall hope was that after quick separation the healing sticks would take over and they would be healed. It was risky nonetheless, but the boys and their parents were willing to take the chance because the boys said they would risk it for a chance at a new life.

I watched intensely and prayed that God would heal them. What a testimony that would be to the world. They did not show any of the surgery on television and I was watching it about eight hours after they were taken into the hospital. So now it was live, waiting for the hospital spokesperson to come out with the results. When the spokesperson came to the microphones you could see a smile on his face. He reported that the separation was a complete success and that both boys were doing fine and were out of danger. The room erupted with a standing ovation as news crews from around the globe reported the most miraculous miracle to date. They would not give any specific details concerning the separation except to say that what they had witnessed was the most astounding miracle in the world.

My heart flooded with praise to the Lord for this mighty display of greatness. I bowed my head and gave glory to Jesus for His goodness and the blood He gave for the healings of the nations. I wondered what could top this, who would have ever even dreamed of trying to do something like this? It goes to show that we, as humans, are wonderfully made; we have so much creativity if only we allow our minds to open up and think things through. It is not by chance these things happen, for chance favors the prepared mind. As with most things in life, the great men are just ordinary men that don't ever stop. They don't tire when the going is rough. I was inspired by these people who went out on a limb and had success.

It wasn't very long after that when Indonesia was having some internal problems because of all the different religions there. It caused uproar because the healing of the Siamese twins came from the cross of Jesus Christ. The religions that didn't profess that they believed in Jesus were not happy over what took place. Some were calling it a hoax and demanding to see the Siamese twins again. They claimed the two boys that were shown were substitutes and not the same boys as before. Another thing that made the other religions mad was that it was Israel who donated the sticks to the twins as a good will gesture of love. Bible scholars that taught on prophecy said this was the beginning of "All that can be shaken will be shaken."

CHAPTER 8

# Walking and Leaping and Praising God

Our wedding day arrived and I was very nervous. Not because I had any doubts, but after all I was thirty-four years old and had never been married. Tracy was thirty-two and she was taking it without a hint of worry. When we said our vows it was not because of a minister standing in front of us. It was our vows we said to each other in front of the living God. A vow means a solemn promise to do something and I had proposed in my heart and to Tracy that I would forever love her as Christ loved the Church. For our honeymoon we went to Hawaii and the surrounding islands. The time on the beach was exquisite; hand in hand watching the sunset was just absolutely captivating. We could never get close to the ocean waters because of my wheelchair so we just went to the edge of the sand. We agreed that since we were both late bloomers we would start a family right away.

Our dreams came to be a reality a few months later when Tracy announced she was pregnant. We were blessed and every night we prayed together to thank the Lord. Tracy was tempting me to take a healing stick because she reasoned that I would never be able to take our baby to play baseball or ride a bike with.

"Honey," I said, "you know the doctor told me I was getting better all the time."

"Yes, I know that, but what if you don't get better for years?" she asked.

"I am feeling stronger every day and I have faith that what God told me would come true!" I responded.

"David, what if the situation were reversed? Would you want me to refuse getting healed?" she questioned.

"Okay, honey, you're right. If it takes longer then the doctor says, we will discuss it again," I said.

"That's fair enough. I just want some hope that one day you will be able to walk again," she replied.

The temptation was taking its toll on me, for I wanted so bad to be able to walk up to Tracy and take her in my arms without having the wheelchair in my way.

About three months after that Tracy became ill and had to be rushed to the hospital. The doctors told us that because she was thirty-two years old she was having complications. After a few days of tests it was determined that unless a miracle happened she was going to have a miscarriage. We were faced with a decision as to what to do. Tracy and I discussed the possibility of giving her a healing stick that I still had left with the federal government. We weren't sure if it would help the baby inside her womb. We didn't know if maybe it would be too much power in her body and actually hurt the baby. "Honey," Tracy said, "don't you think that God would use the healing in a way that wouldn't hurt the baby?"

"With all the healings that have happened around the world, I think that God has designed each need to be met according to whatever is wrong in a person's body!" I replied.

"I think you're right. I guess what troubles me is that you want me to try to give God a chance healing my body with the baby inside and yet you won't give God the chance to heal you?" Tracy stated.

"Please, honey, you know I am waiting on the Lord. If I take a stick now the world will have a heyday with me because my whole reason for not taking one all this time was because I said God told me I would bring Him glory," I begged.

"Okay, I think you're going to be strong in what God told you and I respect you for that. I think we should try a healing stick on me for the sake of our baby, what do you think?" she said.

"I am proud of you for being so understanding after all this time, and I think we should do as you said and just walk by faith that the baby will respond to the healing powers that will flow though your body!" I claimed.

I had to do some finagling the next day to try and get a stick with the federal government. Finally they agreed after much talk and so I sent my jet to go pick it up for time's sake. When the stick was in our hands, we went to the doctor and met him in the hospital to administer the healing. He was fully aware of what we were going to do and he agreed, as this was the only hope to save our baby. The doctor had everything ready to make sure he would be ready in case of any emergency. The baby's heartbeat was extremely weak by now, so there wasn't a minute to spare. Tracy asked me to poke her in the leg with the stick. She didn't want her arm to hurt she said. One, two, three, a jolt went through her and she seemed to be fine.

Quickly the doctor had the Ultrasound in place and the baby's heart was beating normal again. We all breathed a sigh of relief and gratitude to our Lord for this great miracle. I was in total awe that of all the things I had seen, God still was doing marvelous wonders in the world. My heart loved the Lord more than ever and my prayer life had gotten to the point where when I didn't spend time with my Heavenly Father I felt a sense of loneliness. The doctor told us we could go home, but he wanted to check Tracy again tomorrow.

On our way home Tracy drove as usual and we were so happy we sang to the Lord with great joy in our hearts. My marriage was fantastic, both of us loved God so much it was as if He was with us everywhere we went. We acknowledged that sometimes when Tracy and I talked together we would ask Jesus what He thought. The average person watching us would think we were both insane. But that's how far we had come in our oneness with each other and with the Lord. We had chosen the better things of God by giving Him our time and companionship, and in return He gave us His life of abundance.

I remembered a story in the Bible where Jesus came to a village and a woman named Martha invited him over for dinner. Martha was very busy cooking the meal and getting all the preparations ready and when she came out to where Jesus was sitting, there was Mary her sister sitting at the Lord's feet listening to what He had to say. Martha was upset and asked Jesus, "Lord, don't you care that while I am busy doing all the work Mary isn't helping?" The reply astounded her as Jesus said, "Martha, Martha, you are worried and upset about many things, but only one thing is needed. Mary has chosen what is better, and it will not be taken away from her" (Luke 10:41). Mary chose to rest in the Lord and learn from Him and in return Jesus blessed her.

Tracy and I had learned the secret of resting in the Lord Jesus. We knew that no matter what the situation was in our lives, God was here with us to help. We may not always like what happens, like me being in a wheelchair, but He's always by our side to give us comfort in our time of need.

Tracy pulled around to the side of the house to park the car in the shade instead of the garage. I got out and walked to her door and opened it for her.

"David!" she screamed like our car was on fire. Her shriek pierced my heart and it skipped several beats.

"What?" I stammered back.

"You walked! You just walked!" she yelled.

"Oh sweet Jesus!" I screeched. "How did I do that?" I questioned.

"It must be your day! The same day our baby is healed you are healed!" Tracy cried.

"Honey," I shouted, "let me try to walk some more." I sobbed. I started waking around to the back of the car and towards a tree. It wasn't the prettiest sight in the world because I had a funny limp, but I was walking. Without a wheelchair, without a cane or a crutch. My body was moving on its own. I fell down on to my knees under the tree and just started praising God on the top of my lungs. Tracy ran over next to me and we had a church service right there in our front yard. If anybody saw the two of us they would think we needed to be committed the way we carried on. Tears streamed down our faces and gratitude filled our hearts. For today our Savior has saved our baby and made the lame to walk. "Hallelujah!" I shouted. We got up off our knees and I started for the house walking and leaping and praising God.

In the evening Tracy and I decided that it would be beneficial if we took a little walk together to strengthen my legs. We walked and talked together about our plans now that I was able to get around easier. The sun was setting and the color of the sky was a pleasant orange color. As we walked near the tree I saw a baby bird's nest lying on the ground, next to it was a tiny baby bird. The nest must have fallen out of the tree with the helpless bird in it. I walked to the other side of the yard to try to find something to make a home with and the bird followed me. It was odd that he followed me around. I made a nest out of a plastic flowerpot and attached it to the tree with another plastic lid over it in case of rain. I gathered pine needles and leaves and made him a nice cozy little nest. After feeding him some water and bread mixed with milk he was ready for bed. I felt an obligation to the bird because now that I found him I couldn't just leave him alone to die. Tracy told me as we went back inside that I was a softy at heart. "You're going to be a wonderful father," she told me.

The next morning I got a call from my friend who told me that the young boy Michael was having some trouble in a foster home they placed him in. He asked me I knew of any church organizations that could help council the family he was staying with because they felt the boy was depressed. I told him I would see what I could do and he gave me the foster family's phone number. When I told Tracy about the call she wanted to go visit him. So I called the family and they said it would be all right if we came by. When we saw Michael he was excited and said, "You're the healing stick man."

"Oh you remember, Michael," I said.

Tracy asked him how his toy clown was doing and Michael said it was his best friend. We asked the family if we could take him for the day and they said it was okay as long as we called them if he started crying or anything. Off we went to take Michael to the most wonderful day he'd had in a long time. He was such a pleasure to be around and our hearts bonded together.

When the day was coming to an end, Michael said to Tracy and I, "You're just like my mom and dad, we always had fun together too!" It broke our hearts and Tracy had tears streaming down her face. We kissed him and told him we would visit later on.

As we drove away Tracy said, "David, would you ever consider adopting Michael?"

I was taken by surprise because I was just thinking the same thing. "Wow, honey, that's strange. I was just thinking about that!" I told her.

"Then let's try, okay, honey? Do you think we should?" she asked.

"If you think we can with the baby coming and all, I don't have a problem with it," I replied.

Tracy started to make arrangements to get Michael into our family and we prayed that if it were God's will He would make a way.

## BLESSED IS THE ONE WHO READS
## THE WORDS OF THIS PROPHESY

It was getting to be quite busier at work with all that was going on in the world. I was asked to be a corporate sponsor to a national computer chip firm that was on the cutting edge of technology, because this company needed additional funding for a product they deemed of vital interest to the world as a whole. We had a meeting set up for me and my board of directors to meet with this manufacturer to see if we would be interested in their endeavor.

The man in charge of the project was Chris and he was well-versed in contemporary family issues of the time. He asked if he could share his personal thoughts with us and maybe to see if we could join in funding the project that was already complete; they just needed more funds to take it to the general public. "Okay, Chris," I said, "let's hear what you have on your hands."

"Ladies and gentlemen of Fresh Refreshment Company, I want to lay some ground work for my presentation by giving you examples of life today in America concerning our children. As we watch the news every day it seems we are plagued with child abductions. This threat to our society cannot continue is this current direction. Our children's safety is at hand and it is the responsibility of every adult to protect them with whatever means we have at our disposal. Even our newborn babies are at risk of being given to the wrong parents after birth.

"Our company has developed a tiny microchip a little bigger than a grain of rice. We have had similar tests over many years of inserting this type into animals. The results show that no negative health problems have arrived in this widespread testing. Many lost animals have been returned to their owners by the placement of this device in the animal's skin. When a lost animal is picked up, the Humane Society simply scans the animal and it shows the phone number and address of the owners, and it all works out for the best.

"Our company has developed a much more extravagant microchip that will be placed into the hand of each child. This device, which is put into the skin, is simple and virtually painless. The microchip is heat sensitive to the human body and will not have any adverse side effects in regard to health. Because the chip is sensitive to body temperature, in case of death it will send out a distress signal to a global positioning satellite and we can have a track on it within minutes. We have worked with intelligence services to make these chips able to be located with pinpoint accuracy. When a child is kidnapped it would be easy to find his or her location within minutes. We believe this is the answer to worried parents all across America.

"As it has done tremendous good for the dogs and cats around our country, so it will protect our children. The microchip is already being used and has been injected into some people for some time now without flaw. What we are asking this corporation to do is help us fund an advertising campaign that will saturate the entire country with this idea of protecting our beloved children. In return for this sponsorship you will be entitled to partial earnings of our company," Chris spoke elegantly.

I was jolted in my being! My mind raced to the Book of

Revelation where it says, *"He* [the Antichrist] *also forced everyone, small and great, rich and poor, free and slave, to receive a mark on his right hand or on his forehead, so that no one could buy or sell unless he had the mark, which is the name of the beast or the number of his name. This calls for wisdom. If anyone has insight, let him calculate the number of the beast, for it is man's number. His number is 666"* (Revelation 13:16-18).

I knew this was coming for many years now. When all products started to come out with codes to identify them and scanners in grocery stores, I remembered back to my Sunday school lessons in high school. It was a precursor to getting the globe hooked into a system where we could never return to the old way of doing things. It made economical sense. No one argued that and consumers loved the speed in which you could go through the grocery store line and check out. Then the Internet came and everything went online to make ease of transactions of buying without even being in a store. Credit card companies started putting computer chips in the plastic card to move us in to the direction we were talking about today.

"Board," I spoke clearly to everyone, "we have got to take this request and gather more information and let's have a meeting on it next week at this same time," I advised.

"Thank you very much all of you and I will be anxiously waiting for your response," Chris said.

After the meeting Tracy and I went to my office and we were both stunned at what we had just heard. We have been studying Bible prophesy lately together and this was an absolute mind blower. Tracy said the baby was more active than ever as we sat listening to the presentation.

"Honey," she asked, "are you going to give money to sponsor this program?"

"No, I would never be a part of what is the beginning of the mark of the beast," I beamed.

I told the board of directors the same day not to bother looking up any information on the subject because I was not interested in lining up our company with other companies.

# GOD GETS THE GLORY

After my healing, the headlines read, "David Clayton Walks on Water!" and "David Defeats Goliath!" The churches in America were overflowing with great joy of the miracle that God had done for me. This inspired them to keep pressing on for the greatest revival the earth has ever known. It was taking over the world! I was given thousands of flowers that were placed in front of the gates of my house from people everywhere who wanted to show me they cared. My wheelchair was donated to a museum that said they would use it as a piece to show that this great healing took place in our history. Of course my critics were suspicious of how I came to walk again and spread rumors that I used a healing stick. With each piece of evidence that brought glory to God, my critics were following close behind me with negative slander. I told the world that God said He would bring glory to His name if I allowed myself to be used and open with the general public and I did just what He asked of me. All my medical records were open to the public to show the healing was happening over a period of time and not all at once as my critics proclaimed. My reward was me being able to walk again and plus the most beautiful woman in the world by my side.

My mom, Christa and Justin all came to see me after my healing. I never said to any of them, "I told you so." Although Christa never tempted me to use a stick, she had been kind of sad over the whole time I was in the wheelchair and unable to walk. Justin was in great spirits and he was now working for Fresh Refreshment Company and he loved life. Mother was newly energized that I was with Tracy and she was going to be a grandmother soon.

My lawyers completed all the paperwork to adopt Michael and we were ready to bring him home. My mother agreed to stay with us for a while to help him with his new surroundings. Mom's eyes glowed with the prospect of taking care of a child again after all those years. When Michael arrived, his eyes were wide open in astonishment after he came inside the house.

He asked, "Is this my new house, Grandma?"

Mom said, "It's your house. Come, do you want to see your

bedroom?" She had gone on a spending spree to get him everything you could possibly think of. When he saw his new bedroom with everything in it, he went running into the living room shouting, "Mom, Dad, I love you so much!" It touched our hearts to hear him call me dad and Tracy was in tears.

# SAVE THE CHILDREN

A powerful politician was emerging from the Roman Empire. He was thought of as a genius and, I have to admit, a highly intelligent man who got what he wanted. He had a significant following for all the good works he did for the people. No Bible prophesy teacher would come right out and say he was the Antichrist, but you could tell from their dialog that it wasn't an impossibility either. It did seem strange to me that he was on the world scene when the microchip company was putting out advertising to promote their implantable chip into children. After our corporation told them we didn't want to mix with other business dealings, Chris found another corporate giant to fund their goals. Commercials were coming on television explaining the microchip and the benefits to parents. They painted a portrait of being a bad parent who didn't love your children if you did not accept the chip.

Tracy and I had discussed it many times and I told her that in its own way the idea was ingenious. "Think about it," I told her. "If everyone had a chip put in him or her and you couldn't buy or sell anything, you could almost virtually stop crime. If people worked and didn't receive a paycheck but was automatically deposited into an account for you them whenever they went to the store you would just scan your hand and the funds would be drawn out of your account. How would the drug dealers sell drugs? They would have to go back to a bartering method where they would give the drugs in exchange for goods such as cars and other things. It would be virtually impossible to make huge drug deals because money would not be in use anymore. The illegal drug industry would be devastated almost immediately. Theft would go down because there wouldn't be money to sell stolen items for.

"It would all be electronic and if a car was stolen and sold the computers would pick it up instantly. Old people would be helped because purse-snatchers would know they didn't have any money. Burglaries would go down and crime as we know it would be stopped in its tracks. Of course, where there is a will there is a way, and people would work ways around the new system, but overall our world would change. Terrorism would be set back greatly because you could monitor what is being sold and who is buying it. The most captivating lure to the people of America is that if their children were ever kidnapped they could be found in a short amount of time. It sounds like the answer mankind's been waiting for. That's its deception, its the greatest invention of all time, but the result will bring dictatorship and captivity to a world that is now connected to a system that, if controlled by an evil person, could bring our own demise.

"The microchip company coined the name, 'Invisible Money.' They are putting pressure on families in their current advertising blitz that to love your children is to make sure they are safe! It makes sense too, after all, when think about it. You're in a shopping mall and you are distracted looking at clothes. Michael wonders off and next thing you know he's gone. You are frantically yelling at everyone for your son, security shows up and they call the special hotline number. Within a few minutes the police have downloaded the direction the child is headed with global positioning satellites. The abductor is arrested and you go home safely with Michael!" I exclaimed wildly.

"Unbelievable," Tracy responded. "These sure are the signs of the times we've been reading about."

"I'm not going down without a fight though," I told Tracy. "I'm going to get my own group together and counter attack this massive guilt trip they're putting on parents. I will use the 'Big Brother is Watching Over You' campaign. I will tell the parents that the system can work two ways and predators will come up with their own system and they will be able to tell where your children are at all times. Fear can work in reverse too! I'll tell the parents this is just the start of your invasion of privacy and later you will be made to have a chip placed in your body or you won't be able to work or earn any money. How would you feel if you were in the privacy of your own bedroom and global positioning satellites could pinpoint your closeness to one another? I will spread the word that what we need is to put such a device on those who are caught doing harm to children only. I will reverse the onslaught of mud being thrown on parents who don't like what is about to come. Tracy, what do you think, should I throw millions of my own dollars into this to wake the world up?" I asked.

"David, we're getting ready to have our baby soon, what would you think if it was mandatory to have the baby implanted right after birth!" Tracy lashed out.

"Honey, you're absolutely right. I think I married a cute little genius here," I replied. I was ready to embark on a mission to spread the word that this system doesn't bring freedom it brings bondage.

* * *

My baby bird had to be fed several times a day. I had gone to a pet store and bought bird-feeding stuff for babies. It was a lot of responsibility for a man as busy as myself. I had a wife and a new son, a baby on the way any day, and now a hungry baby bird to feed. Besides that I had to hire a political advertising firm that knows how to fight to stop the spread of Invisible Money's brain washing.

"Lord," I prayed while climbing up a ladder to feed the bird, "maybe I'm in over my head here, I've already been shot at twice, hit with bullets twice, crippled and maimed. I've been publicly stomped on; I've been sued in court here in America and other countries too. My life has been an open book with no privacy and now I'm ready to take on the devil? How much more should I do?" I asked.

An answer came to me from deep within my soul. "My dear child, you are chosen to be my ambassador, you have brought the world my healing power and have witnessed the greatest revival of all time," the Lord spoke.

"Yes, Father, but I'm so weak," I claimed.

"My son, in your weakness I am strong. Do you see this baby bird with his beak wide open for you to put food into it?" God asked.

"Yes, Lord, I do," I replied.

"I put this tiny bird in your life to show you about myself, just as the bird is dependent upon you to keep it safe and alive, so I want you to be dependent on me for all the things that are just ahead," God said.

"Yes, dear Lord Jesus, I will give myself unto you and submit my life to your plan," I promised.

"With you I am very pleased," the Lord stated.

Just then the tiny bird started to chirp as if to say thank you for feeding me. I went inside and told Tracy what the Lord said to me. Tracy knew that God was faithful and would guide me in His good timing. Michael was running around playing and my mom was having the time of her life with him.

# CHAPTER 9
# He Who has an Ear Let Him Hear

Our battle for the air raged on with my campaign against Invisible Money. I think the population would have been more easily taken in at this time by the deception to save the children. But the most convincing thing that gave people faith was all the many miracles they had seen around them. There was a spiritual battle being fought and it was going on right in front of our eyes. I knew that all these years that children who were being kidnapped and coming up missing was for a reason. The devil was pushing for parents to live in fear regarding their children. Year after year it got worse to the point of parents buying dog chains to put on their children. The news pounded away whenever a child was missing, and even though this did sometimes help find children, it also brought on great amounts of stress.

The government came out with the "Amber Alert" system, which was named after a child who had gone missing. This system would bring massive radio and television coverage to the area when a child came up lost. It was successful so far and I praised such programs and felt they were great for the battle for our children's safety. But now the government itself was siding up with Invisible Money to put a chip in every child.

With healings still dominating the headlines in world events, and God being the most talked about subject of our day, the Church started to find itself in muddy water. The majority of churches were against "tagging" our children. So even though the Church was in its greatest revival of all time and triumph unspeakable. They were starting to see a persecution rising up against them for their stance against the issue of the safety of implanting our children with microchips. My campaign was making its point, but fear was a bigger motivator and people became frightened at the images they were slashing across the television screen. The commercials showed abductors stalking children and this sent shockwaves of fear through parents.

A credit card company had come out with a thumbprint credit card. When you wanted to buy something and charge it you had to place your thumb on a square box on the credit card and the cashier had thirty seconds to run it through the slider. The credit card "knew" each person's thumbprint so this stopped illegal credit card use, at least for the customers of that credit card company.

With all this going on in the world, I was entirely dependent on God for my strength. Jesus said, "When these things begin to take place, stand up and lift your heads, because your redemption is drawing near" (Luke 21:28). That night, as I soundly slept, Tracy woke me up with news her water had broken. We had everything packed and prepared to go to the hospital just for the occasion. My mom stayed with Michael and we went to the hospital with me driving like a madman. Tracy was breathing hard when we arrived and we were whisked off into the ward for births.

"Honey," Tracy called, "whatever we have, boy or girl, I want you to know I love you!"

"I love you too, sweetheart!" I responded.

"Please never leave my side, okay?" she asked.

"I promise, honey, you will always be my love," I stated. She was squeezing my hand so tight it was turning white. The time was near and Tracy was sweating profusely. Within a half hour, Tracy let out a yell and out came our beautiful baby girl. "Honey, we have a girl!" I shouted.

"Thank you, David, for being my true love," Tracy bellowed.

The doctor handed her our little girl and Tracy's face was filled with the sunshine of God, beaming from her gratefulness. A nurse asked us if we had a name picked out. We had settled on picking one of three names and instantly we both said at the same time "Jean!" My sister Christa loved the name Jean too and so I knew she would be ecstatic! The nurse laughed and said that at least we had the same thoughts. The most unusual thing was that Jean had a lot of hair already. I was thinking silently, *It must be because of the healing sticks. It gave Jean an extra dose of hair.* I spent the whole day there with Tracy, and Mom came by with Michael to see the new baby. Michael was star struck by her; he had never seen such a small baby before.

"Dad," he said, "will she be next to my room so I can play with her?"

"Of course, we fixed up the room next to yours, remember?" I replied. I don't think seeing the room fixed up and now seeing a baby made him grasp that the baby was what was in his mommy's stomach.

"Oh yeah," he giggled.

When it came time to bring mom and Jean home, I put up banners in the house and wooden storks in the front yard. As we drove up into the driveway, Michael asked, "Dad, where did the big birds come from?"

"They are storks, Michael, to welcome home your mom and your new little sister," I told him. He thought they were real. We had our hands full for the next couple of days and so I had our cook from my jet liner come over and stay in the guesthouse for a few days to help get us through. Mother was in heaven eating gourmet meals three times a day. "I may never go home!" she promised.

## THE MAN OF SIN

Daniel was getting stronger. He was calling on all Europe to back him in his efforts to revolutionize the world, as he called it. He was waging his own campaign of war for microchips to be the system that replaced money. He used the same arguments we were hearing over in America: how this would bring the world complete prosperity. He said that trade with other nations would become easier if we are went to a computer-controlled type of monetary system. Web sites that reported Rapture timetables were at the brink of showing we were at the very threshold of God's next big event. They never would set any dates, but the signs of the times were definitely wavering over us like dark clouds about to burst.

Daniel's ideas were extreme in nature. He had this vision of the whole world living in peace and he taught that this could only come with a government that was global in scope. Even with all this going on, the Church didn't think the Tribulation period was starting because the Rapture hadn't happened. The Rapture is the event when Jesus comes to take His people home and we all are instantly transformed into heaven. I agreed with this way of thinking because even though this man was mighty in his nature, the events of the end time were not in place yet for the Antichrist to take over the world scene.

I believed we were at the time in scripture when Jesus says, "Watch out that no one deceives you. For many will come in my name, claiming, 'I am the Christ,' and will deceive many. You will hear of wars and rumors of wars, but see to it that you are not alarmed. Such things must happen, but the end is still to come" (Matthew 24:4-6). The television networks were even having guest speakers on to talk about prophetic events. God was using the strongholds of Satan to make known His love for the whole human race. The nations of the world did seem to be lining up in a way that was militaristic in manner. In other words, the nations were trying to fortify themselves from each other by placing themselves in a strategic line up.

Israel, being in the most vulnerable position of all, was going through its own internal struggle. They'd had so many healings take place that it was hard to deny that the cross of Jesus Christ healed them. Many people danced in the streets thinking that the return of the Messiah must be coming soon because God has brought them such a great gift. Most of the population did not accept that the cross found was from Jesus and they denied that any healing was because Jesus died on that cross. They agreed that they had witnessed wonderful miracles, but it was not Jesus who made them happen for He was dead, rather it was just God who brought the miracles.

It reminded me of the time in the Bible when Jesus was healing many people and the religious leaders were up in arms over what He was doing. The Pharisees were plotting against Jesus. A demon-possessed man was brought before Jesus who was blind and mute and Jesus healed him. The man started talking and was able to see again. Some of the people asked if Jesus could be the son of David. When the Pharisees heard that Jesus had performed this great miracle, they said it had to be that he did this by the power of Beelzebub. Jesus reply to them was, "Every kingdom divided against itself will be ruined, and every city or household divided against itself will not stand. If Satan drives out Satan, he is divided against himself. How then can his kingdom stand? And if I drive out demons by Beelzebub, by whom do your people drive them out? So then, they will be your judges. But if I drive out demons by the Spirit of God, then the kingdom of God has come upon you" (Matthew 12:25-28). I think that the many healings taking place in Israel will be the judge, and if so, just like the scripture says, the kingdom of God has come upon you. Sometimes the most hardhearted people are the ones who see the greatest of miracles.

In the life story of Moses, when he went before Pharaoh to try to get the Pharaoh to let the Israelites go free, great miracles were done through Moses and Aaron. Plagues were sent to down to help Pharaoh with his decision. The Israelites watched as God turned water into blood. He sent frogs that covered the land, along with gnats and flies. Moses bugged Pharaoh and he bugged him, but Pharaoh was hardened. Livestock was killed, the Egyptians had boils, and they had hail rain down. Locusts came from everywhere and to top it off the firstborn son of each family in Egypt died. You would think that if you were witnessing these events at that time that the people would have said, "Wow, God is in control and I believe He will do what is right for us."

When the armies of Egypt chased the Israelites they were in a jam because the Red Sea was in front of them and the armies of Egypt behind them. They grumbled to Moses and said that Moses should have just left them in Egypt to die. But God did a great miracle and they were all able to cross over on dry land as the waters turned into a great wall. Once they reached the other side, God closed the water and the whole Egyptian army drowned. That would increase the faith of anybody, right? Not necessarily.

The Lord then led them with a pillar of cloud in the day, and after they became thirsty and didn't find any water for three days, they grumbled. When they did find some water it was bitter and they couldn't drink from it. When Moses cried out to God for help, God showed Moses a piece of wood and when Moses threw it into the water, the water became sweet for the children of Israel to drink. I like that story because God used a piece of wood to give them water and save them, and here—right now in our generation—God was again using a piece of wood to show His glory to all the earth! That fascinated me and I had to praise the Lord when I thought about it.

Later on the Israelites were reminiscing about the food they had in Egypt because they were hungry so God sent them food, which appeared each day on the ground. It must have been health food if it was God who gave it to you directly. But as usual they soon tired of the manna and grumbled again. As they traveled through the desert continuing their journey, God had a pillar of fire at night for them to see their way to the Promised Land. Then when they needed more water on their continuing journey, Moses struck a rock in the middle of the desert and water came out for them.

You would think that after witnessing all these fantastic miracles right in front of them they would believe that God would be able to do anything for them. But when they got to the area right before the Promised Land and saw the enemy was bigger and stronger than them, they grumbled and complained again. When Caleb and Moses told the people they could overtake the land, this was their response: "We can't attack those people; they are stronger than we are"

(Numbers 13:31). So after wondering in the wilderness all this time, they were right on the threshold of claiming what they traveled for and they wouldn't trust God who had done great and marvelous miracles right before their unbelieving eyes.

Joshua, who had went into the land and saw it, told them it was a land flowing with milk and honey. He was so irate that the Israelites were again complaining he tore his clothes and said, "The land we passed through and explored is exceedingly good. If the Lord is pleased with us, he will lead us into that land, a land flowing with milk and honey, and will give it to us" (Numbers 14:8). Still the Israelites wanted to stone their leaders. God Himself had to intervene and said to Moses, "How long will they refuse to believe in me, in spite of all the miraculous signs I have performed among them?" (Numbers 14:11).

God was disappointed; what on earth would it take for them to trust in Him? Just like the people today who were seeing this great outpouring of God's grace, I wondered what else they needed to see. So God told Moses He was going to strike them down with a plague and destroy them. He still promised Moses that He would make him into a great nation though. Moses had to reason with God that if He did this then everybody would hear about it and they would say that God was not able to bring the children of Israel into the land that had been promised them by an oath and instead God slaughtered them in the desert. The Lord then forgave them again. It kind of makes you wonder, what else did God need to show them so that they could trust in Him?

Was it still the same today in Israel? In spite of the overpowering miracles that had been done right before their eyes, many still did not believe. I was hoping there was time for them and even though many in Israel turned to Jesus for their salvation, mostly it was business as usual. I reasoned with God, as did Moses when he asked God to spare the Israelites. "Father, please be patient with your children and be merciful once again as you have always been. I will be a voice to them if it be your will, O'God. I will go to them and be your mouthpiece if it pleases you, Lord," I prayed in earnest.

# THANKFUL HEARTS

My new baby girl and son were doing great. Tracy was looking as beautiful as ever and she was the sweetest mom to the children. Our love had flourished even more in the last few weeks and I could not comprehend ever living without her. I was praying and reading my Bible in my study and I wondered why God waited all those years to give her to me. Then I realized God didn't wait all those years, I did! I laughed out loud over the thought and many times as I read my Bible I laughed at the humor that God shows in His word. The times I spent in His presence were exhilarating and I loved this time alone getting to know my creator. It's funny how when things happen in our life we tend to blame God, especially if it is something bad, but when something good happens to us we forget about the great answer that came from Him.

Jesus was on His way to Jerusalem. As He was passing through a village there were ten men and each of them had leprosy. The men yelled to Jesus as He was passing them by, "Master, have mercy and compassion on us." Jesus just told them to go and show themselves to the priests and as they did they were healed. One of the ten men came back to Jesus praising God, and running up to bow down at His feet, he thanked the Lord. He was a Samaritan. I think this must have surprised Jesus as he said to the man, "Were not all ten cleansed? Where are the other nine? Was no one found to return and give praise to God except this foreigner?" Then He said to him, "Rise and go; your faith has made you well" (Luke 17:17).

When we really think about it we are ungrateful people. We take everything for granted. We think the world owes us a living and we get mad at God if life doesn't work things out the way we think He should. Many people give tithes and think that now God owes them something; whether this is true or not is not the point. You can give all you want, but if you are still ungrateful in your heart and have an unthankful attitude, God knows. You can't trick God! He knows that the more you have the more you think you need. God knows the heart of all mankind and just as Jesus questioned where the other nine were, He questions still today.

What if you had a child and you gave them everything they asked for and they never appreciated what they had nor did they take care of it, would you keep giving and giving? I had a friend who was desperate for a car a few years ago and would have taken anything at the time. Somehow he was able to get an almost new car that had low mileage and was in great shape. When I saw him a few years later he still had the same car, but he told me he didn't like it anymore. When I asked him if he was having trouble with it he said no and that he just didn't like it. That is the unthankfulness of man to God. We ask, we pray, we plead for things and a few years or even days later we are unsatisfied. Don't we think that God sees our hearts? When we go to pray for something else we want, who's to say that God doesn't think, "why should I give you a new car when you never appreciated the one I gave you in the first place?" Many of us tend not to understand the thoughts of God and that simply is because we really don't completely one hundred percent believe in Him!

Let me ask you this: Do you honestly believe that in a heaven somewhere there is this all-powerful God? Do you believe that God knows the hearts of all of us? If you really, honestly believe that God is in heaven and He watches our lives, then why don't you take the time to get to know Him?

"What are you talking about?" you reply. "I go to church twice a week!" My answer to that is spend an hour with your husband or wife twice a week and see what happens. You're not fooling God, He knows your thoughts. I am not saying this to bother you or scare you, but the fact of the matter is that God created people so we would have companionship with Him. Many people think they are holier than other people because they go to church regularly. Going to church is not the only thing God wants, He wants you. He wants your heart and He wants to have a relationship with all His creation.

The Bible says, "Come now, let us reason together, says the Lord" (Isaiah 1:18). One meaning of reason is to talk logically. Jesus also said come and let us sup together. That word sup means to eat an evening meal. When you eat together you talk and get to know each other or ask about the day that each of you had. God wants our love, but like the ten lepers we take what we can get and go our way without ever thinking to give Him thanks. We want God to give, but we don't want to give Him back our time? It is the strangest thing to me because my love for God burns in me and drives me to want to meet with Him whenever I can.

Think of anyone you could have come stay with you for a day. The president, your favorite singer or your favorite movie star. You would give anything for one of them to actually come to your house and spend time getting to know you, wouldn't you? Yet, here is God who has made Himself available for anyone who wants Him and we don't come. Yea, but my favorite singer has three gold records, you say. So what, God walks on gold and He has made the universe that has billions of galaxies. Imagine that and then to think that Jesus said if we draw near to him He would draw near to us. The plain and sad truth is that we really don't believe in God enough or our relationship with Him would be the greatest thing in our life! Many people would not have a clue about the word of God if it were not for hearing it from church. Don't you want to know for yourself what God has to say and what His personality is like?

Many times I am lying flat on my stomach in the bedroom praying and getting to know my creator personally and I can tell you it is the greatest time in my life. When I read my Bible and I come across something that Jesus said that is funny to me I start laughing. Tracy asks me what I'm laughing at, and I explain to her what I was reading. God has a sense of humor and He sometimes does things in our life that are quite humorous. When I look back at my life there are many things that have happened that are just plain hysterical and it is a joy when we know God personally and we are able to see His hands on our lives. If you are missing that, then you are missing the greatest thing to ever happen in your life!

It is a wonderful gift to have a marriage with a woman that lets me be myself just as God lets us be ourselves. Tracy doesn't have to tell me every step I take. She knows that I know when something needs to be done. She doesn't have to wake me up in the morning screaming at the top of her lungs for me to do something. She knows I'll do it and we have that respect for each other that allows each of us to have our own life within a life. I can be in our office room reading or studying and she can be out in the living room doing something and she doesn't always have to have my one hundred percent attention. At times she'll often come skipping into the office to give me a big kiss.

I can turn her adult woman's mind into child's playful mind by just saying something silly to her and next thing I know she is dancing and playing around like a young girl. This is the beauty of being free of a life of bitterness and arguments. This is a life of unselfishness where Tracy lets me go where I need to go, no questions asked. As a result of this trust our life together has become almost like a fairytale. When you hover over your mate like a watchdog your mate may bite you back. The last chapter of Proverbs says, "A wife of noble character who can find? She is worth far more than rubies. Her husband has full confidence in her and lacks nothing of value" and again, "Her children arise and call her blessed; her husband also, and he praises her" (Proverbs 31: 10-11, 28).

Do you know how you can tell if your husband has this type of love for his wife or wife for her husband? It's usually by how much time he or she spends with you, at home or going out together. Maybe if he would rather be other places where you're not, you need to become a person that he desires more and visa-versa. Of course there are always situations that force this to be, such as careers where many hours are essential or your husband is in the NBA and travels to five states a week playing basketball. Overall, these are the exceptions and not the rule. This is the connection I'm trying to get across to you about God, how much time is spent together?

The Bible says, "For this reason a man will leave his father and mother and will be united to his wife, and the two will become one flesh" (Ephesians 5:31). We've heard that scripture before, but the most excellent thing is what it says next. "This is a profound mystery—but I am talking about Christ and the church" (Ephesians 5:320). That's incredible! Right when Paul is talking about the relationship between husbands and wives, he throws in that he is also talking about Christ and the Church. You see, God wants to have this same type of relationship with you that a man and a woman should have together. I wrote a simple poem that puts it in perspective. "As man is for woman and woman for man, when a sinner comes to Jesus he's made whole again." God longs for your love and He desires for a relationship with each human being on the planet Earth. The question remains, how will we respond to this call?

God as a loving Father shows us things He wants us to know about Him and when God relates to us in this way it brings great joy. The more God shows us the more we should want to learn of Him and that brings a satisfying life free from trying to find happiness in pleasures of the world. If your sense of peace in your life is coming from your mate, your friends or your children then you will lead a miserable life because people will let you down and you'll be discouraged. On the other hand, when you realize that your peace and joy in life comes from knowing whom you are in Christ, then you can have calmness in the midst of life's storms. Peter said, "His divine power has given us everything we need for life and godliness through our knowledge of him who called us by his own glory and goodness" (2 Peter 1:3). That's why most people are very unhappy because it is only through God that we can be content.

I went into a pet store one day to buy some fish and I asked them if I bought a certain fish if it would outgrow the tank I had. The pet store employee told me that a fish can only grow according to the size of the tank they're in! What size tank are you in? Are you limiting your life to places and friends that will keep you in a small fish bowl? How about your mind? Just because you haven't been the kind of person who seeks God, does that mean you always have to stay that way? I have experienced things from God that are amazing and my life is full because of what I know. Throw yourself into the ocean of vast learning and get out of your restricted desktop fish bowl!

# CHAPTER 10
# Behold,
# I Stand at the Door

The world situation was still in the euphoria of being blessed by the healings, and massive numbers of people were giving their lives to God. Not just in America but all across the whole world. The tiny nation of Haiti was having the most wonderful revival imaginable and people believed God for miracles and miracles were happening daily. If I were to try to write all of them down it would be impossible to record them all. Television stations were still showing the things that God was doing and it seemed finally safe for children to watch television without seeing sex and non-stop violence. The world was truly a wonderful place at this time in spite of the negative aspects. Millions of people were having unprecedented revival even though the computer chip company was still gearing up for the "greatest thing to happen to the human race" campaign. At least that's what they advertised with the Invisible Money deal.

On the other side of the world was "Daniel," as he called himself, and he was staunch about not letting anybody use his last name. Many believed he had an obsession with the Daniel in the Old Testament because Nebuchadnezzar took Daniel captive to Babylon and eventually Daniel was given a high position in Nebuchadnezzar's kingdom. He said he wanted everybody to call him Daniel because the public needed to see him as though he were a brother who cared for them. His beliefs were so extreme and radical it was causing worry among a great number of people. He was greatly loved by many and greatly hated by many. His ideas of bringing the world together weighed heavy on some Christians while others took it as the soon coming of the Lord Jesus Christ. No one would still yet say for sure if this man were the Antichrist spoken about in the book of Revelation. We always knew that if he were the Antichrist then before he started to do any major events as foretold in the book of Revelation, the Rapture of the Church would take place. As of now there were no signs of proof of whom he was.

He had even been trying to get involved in the Middle East peace treaty that America coined the "Road Map to Peace." He wanted the Europeans along with himself to get the peace deal they had worked out into line instead of this road map. Ironically, Israel did not turn away from this offer; they accepted it and this was the beginning of Israel's pull away from America and their leaning toward trusting Europe for their security. Armed with this good news of Israel's invitation for him to get involved, Daniel opened up an office for his staff in Jerusalem. The Lord's return was knocking on the door of civilization. Israel had its hands busy with homicide bombings and the unbelievable number of healings taking place. This was the commencing of the pot being stirred for European involvement into the affairs of Israel.

# ISRAEL I ADORE THEE

I got an invitation from Israel to go back and receive a prestigious award. Because of the overwhelming healings taking place, some people wanted to show their appreciation to me. I have always stressed to the general public everywhere I traveled that it was God's gift to the world and I was just a servant. I never wanted anybody to think I had some great connection with these healings taking place. I was just as shocked as was everybody else when I witnessed the mighty power of God. Tracy begged me not to go. "After all," she said, "we just had a baby."

"Honey," I said, "God has given me this chance to witness to the people of Israel and I need to go."

"I know you do, but I'm worried for you because of all the homicide bombings and terrorist plots happening in Israel," she quivered.

"Honey, I'm sure God will keep me safe for you and the children," I spoke confidently.

"I will pray for you because I know you have a great love for Israel and your heart has always been in Jerusalem," Tracy replied.

I had my jet scheduled for the trip and my bags packed. My heart ached in leaving Tracy behind. The children were too young to understand so it was easier to go. I was called to show the people of Israel God's love.

When I arrived in Israel, I was given a hero's welcome. I felt that same wonderful feeling that I have always felt when I'm in Israel. My spirit soaked up the awe-inspiring glory that overshadowed the Land of Abraham, Isaac and Jacob. I wrote this little poem and placed it in a local newspaper to try to open the eyes of the citizens of Israel. I didn't put my name on it for certain reasons because I felt it should be unknown; I titled it "Pass the Nails."

*Pass the nails from generation to generation and the scar of our sins to our children's children. Pass the nails we hammered them in, we hammered them in with our own sin. A spear was thrown, lots were casts, and an evil world could be freed at last. A crown of thorns, blood on His face, a man marred beyond recognition by a world of hate.*

*Darkness spread over the land, the veil was torn in two, and after three days underground they found an empty tomb. We inherited the world like a rebellious child and we turned away instead. We've used and abused the forgiveness he sent, we misbehaved the love he gave. Now we're unaware that we keep on passing the nails to future generations.*

I was invited to speak at a Christian church in Jerusalem, so when they called me up I had prepared a short sermon that I thought might be good for the church to remember. When I went up to the front I was kind of scared how they would take my message, but it was all I wrote so I had to say what I prepared. This was my sermon.

"I want to thank the people and especially the Christians of Israel for inviting me back to this great country. I prepared a short story and I hope you will all enjoy it. As we read in Acts chapter 20, we find a short but interesting story about a man named Eutychus. Paul left Philippi and sailed into a city called Troas. Now on the first day of the week, the disciples came together to break bread. Paul preached to them and it continued on until midnight.

"There sat on a window ledge a young man named Eutychus. He, like you and I would do, sat there listening to Paul with great interest and faith as Paul preached the gospel of the Lord Jesus Christ. As the night got older, Eutychus began to get sleepy. He tried hard to keep his eyes open, until finally he fell fast asleep. Now Eutychus had been sitting on a windowsill on the third floor of the building where Paul was preaching. When he sunk down into a deep sleep, he fell out the window, down three stories, onto the ground.

"Paul, hearing this great thud, hurried down the stairs with everyone else and there was Eutychus lying dead on the ground. Paul embraced him and probably asked God to spare this young man's life and within moments his eyes opened and he was alive again. They all walked up back to the room and continued breaking bread and thanking God for the great miracle that had just happened.

"We can relate our lives to the story of Eutychus; we sometimes get weary and tired from everyday life. We lose the first love that God gave us when we first got saved. We read too many books and start replacing our Bible reading time with great Christian books. We get caught up in life's fast pace and we don't have the time to pray anymore. As our lives get harder we get wearier and close our eyes a little at a time and soon we fall fast asleep.

"Some of us, like Eutychus, will die not ever coming to the knowledge that we could have known God personally if only we had taken the time. The faith we once had will start to lose its power and our love will grow cold.

"The Christian walk is one of peace and joy all along the way, but if we start to close our eyes soon we will fall asleep and fall back into our old ways and eventually find ourselves dead. I'm not talking about losing salvation here, but rather I am talking about being dead in a relationship that should be alive and filled with great joy. Thank God the faith of Paul was strong enough to believe that God would raise Eutychus from the dead. Remember Proverbs that said: 'A little sleep, a little slumber, a little folding of the hands to rest—and poverty will come on you like a bandit and scarcity like an armed man' (Proverbs 24:33-34). Now this applies to our spiritual lives as well when we don't sit attentively and we start to slumber. Before you know it we are sound asleep and die. Our relationship with Jesus dries up and we become cranky old Christians.

"If you find you are weary, don't close your eyes and fall asleep. Instead go back to the beginning and start all over. Remember how when you first came to Jesus how easy it was to trust Him? Revelation chapter three says: 'Remember, therefore, what you have received and heard; obey it, and repent. But if you do not wake up, I will come like a thief, and you will not know at what time I will come to you' (Revelation 3:3). The time for you is now, strengthen what remains.

"Go back to the Lord and believe with the faith and love you had at the beginning. God has brought the people of Israel a great blessing and He is calling you back to Him. Seek Him while He may be found and take the time you need in prayer and reading to get your first love back into your hearts again. I think this is a good reminder for all of us, myself included, because for many years I turned away from God also. He was steadfast in His love and so because of what I saw I went back to Him, for His love is great. You can do the same starting today.

"The pastor will lead us in prayer now. I thank all of you for giving me the time to speak my heart with you. Remember I love you, and will always keep the people of Jerusalem close to my heart. For

I love the land of Israel as most Christians around the world love Israel and hold her dear to our hearts."

There was a great response to what I had spoken that day and the church said they felt like they were re-energized after the sermon. I only hoped that the things I said would not offend anyone, but I hoped what I said would bring them closer to God. I was not a preacher, just a businessman who lately was not really a businessman either. It was a good thing my firm was self-reliant in running itself thanks to my managerial staff.

The uprisings around neighboring countries of Israel were getting worse. There was fear that because Israel had the healing sticks they would start a war to get more land and oil. Rumors spread that the surrounding hostile nations of Israel would band together and attack God's tiny nation. The talk that Israel wanted to start a war was all unnecessary though because I'd had many talks with the high-ranking government officials of Israel and their only desire was to be left alone so they could live their lives in peace. Some anti-Jewish states in the Middle East were claiming that the healing sticks were a fraud and that it was a Jewish lie. They had asked for a few more sticks to prove it to themselves, but the Israeli government knew that even if they gave them more sticks these countries wouldn't show the true results anyways. They would fabricate some distorted message to their people and try to make them rise up in hatred all the more. The funny thing is that Israel had given the surrounding countries sticks already and they'd had great healings. They wanted more and Israel was afraid they would just show someone who didn't get healed to try to make America and Israel look like liars.

Bible prophecy teachers believed that the cross and the healings that were taking place were God's last call to the world before the Rapture of the Church. I think that I was convinced of this too because the things that were going on around the globe were too unusual. Some churches were even reporting increased healing miracles taking place even without any healing sticks. Great men of God spoke to the world asking for freedom of religion in countries where they persecute believers. Revival blazed on like the end was near.

# PAUL IN CHAINS

While in Israel I tried to visit places where Jesus had walked. It was so amazing to realize that two thousand years ago Jesus was born in a manger and as an adult actually walked with men. The thought of God coming down to earth in the flesh of a human body was staggering. How could we not all see what took place here in this land so long ago? I hoped that the cross would be the miracle that opened the eyes of the Jewish people. Many eyes were opened, but still many could not come to see Christ even with healings taking place right in front of them because their eyes were blinded.

When Jesus walked the earth he healed a man with leprosy, a paralytic, and cast out demons right in front of them yet in Matthew 12:38, the Pharisees and teachers of the law said they wanted to see a miraculous sign from him. Jesus's reply was that they were a wicked and adulterous generation and the only sign He would give them would be the sign of Jonah. Of course He was talking about His death of three days in the grave before he rose again. Like Jonah in the belly of the great fish for three days. Jesus did many miracles right in front of them and yet they asked for signs. I wondered why they would do the same this day and age after witnessing all the healings that were taking place with the healing sticks.

I strolled back to my hotel room with guards by my side and I took in an early night because tomorrow I had plans to go into areas of Israel where many of the attacks against Israel came from. I woke up feeling good and having a positive mental attitude about life. With a small group of people we headed out after breakfast to visit the different areas. We were driving in a van going down a highway that I'd seen on the news before where homicide bombers blew themselves up inside public buses. I shuddered at the thought of people being blown up just because that day they took the bus.

Nearing the place of our visit, a car pulled alongside of us, with machine guns drawn out the windows, demanding us to stop. The driver of the van obeyed, thinking maybe it was for security reasons and they just wanted to talk to us. When we stopped they stormed our van like bees chasing a boy who had stolen their honeycomb. The leader spoke saying he was looking for David Clayton.

"Here I am," I responded and they quickly grabbed me and pulled me out of the van and stuffed me into their car, which looked as though it would break down any minute. It was rusty and had holes all over it. Inside it was plated with heavier steel to try to protect the riders in the car. When I asked the men where we were going, I was punched in the mouth and the left side of my face felt like it was the size of a grapefruit. Blood gushed out of my mouth and one of the men said in broken English, "I'll bet you wish you had one of your healing sticks now," and they all laughed.

The others in the van were taken to a different place than me. I was blindfolded although I don't know why because I had no clue where I was anyways. We drove along bumpy roads for about an hour before stopping. Once we stopped they dragged me out of the car and took me blindfolded into some kind of house. We walked down a long set of stairs so I knew I was going underground. I heard steel gates and chains opening and I was thrown on the ground. I was told not to make any noise or they would gag me and tie me up. When I took off my blindfold there was no one there but me. Here I was sitting in a small jail-type cell in the middle of nowhere and I couldn't see very well because it was kind of dim in the cell.

What I didn't know at the time was they were kidnapping me in hopes of getting some healing sticks from Israel. I was left alone the whole day until night came and it was so dark in the cell I couldn't even see my hand in front of me. The darkness could be felt; it was incredible to be able to feel darkness. I heard some people coming down to where I was and with the best English they could muster up they mocked me.

"So you are the great King David," they snarled. "You think you are some kind of healer, don't you! Well look at you now, Mr. American. Who are you now?" they taunted. "You thought you were some kind of God, huh, do Gods sit in stinking prison cells? These sticks of yours will be ours or else you will die, do you understand, American?"

I didn't answer back because I was afraid and I couldn't see anything anyways. All I could do was listen to them talk. As they kept talking I decided to answer them and so I told them that the healing power from the cross came from the blood of Jesus Christ that was shed for them also. I told them that probably as the blood soaked into the wood, that's what brought about the healings they saw now. I asked them why they had developed such hatred towards the Jewish people and they didn't answer me back. I told them that after the great flood there was only Noah and his family, so that makes all of us brothers. This enraged one of them and I heard him say he was going to kill me, but another man held him back. I asked him what it was that Jesus had done to them to make them not believe.

"Who said we didn't believe in Jesus?" one of them countered.

"Then if you believe in Jesus why are you doing this to me?" I questioned.

"Because we want some healing sticks," he yelled in madness.

I told them the story of Martin Luther King in America and how he went about reform, but in a peaceful manner and that it worked and ultimately black people were given equality. I told them that maybe what they needed was a leader that would not teach their children hatred but rather peace and that would get them further ahead. Instead of making enemies with the people of Israel, maybe by trying to work with them it would bring about what they desired.

One of the men said they had no control because the leadership was leading them in this direction. He asked me to pray for them and I told him I would. I told them that the way they were going was not helping them and that the Bible says, "I will bless those who bless you, and whoever curses you I will curse" (Genesis 12:3). This scripture was talking about Israel. I told them that they were bringing on themselves a curse from God and that's why their cities looked liked crumbling slums. I asked them to give peace a chance and see what would happen.

The one who wanted to kill me still wanted to kill me more, but the other man seemed to listen and acted curious about what I told him. I found out later that while I was in the cell the others in the van were taken away and shot in the head execution style. They demanded from Israel that they give them ten thousand sticks or else I would be killed.

This put the Israeli government in a precarious situation because they did not want to appear weak if they gave in to the demands. News of my kidnapping spread through the world at the speed of light. The American government wanted to send special ops to the area and get me out. Israel didn't want any interference for fear that I would be killed. There were behind the scenes talks between Israel and America, but nobody knew at the time what was going on. The haters in the world were happy about my predicament. All I could do was sit in my cell and hope and pray that God would protect me. I wasn't afraid to die, but I didn't want to die in a dungeon at the hands of low-life criminals who had no decency.

The churches around the world were praying for my safe return. Tracy and my mother found out about it while watching the news and she called my sister Christa and told her about my capture. All of them got together and went to church with a group of women to pray that God would somehow deliver me and bring me back home safely. There were groups of people in churches all over the world praying that God would spare my life.

I tried not to be overcome with anxiety because I remembered when Paul was in prison he wrote a lot of the New Testament while under lock and key. I remembered the story of how the Church, shortly after of the death of Jesus, was praying for the Apostle Peter who was put into prison during the persecution of the church. King Herod saw that it pleased the Jews, so he had James the brother of John put to death by the sword and then he proceeded to arrest Peter also. Peter was thrown into prison and guarded by four squads of four soldiers each. Herod's plans were to bring Peter to trial. The night before the trial Peter was sleeping. Two soldiers were guarding him and he was bound with two chains. Guards stood at the entrance of the jail. A miracle happened when God sent an angel into Peter's cell and told him to stand up and walk out. Peter walked out of the jail cell following the angel. Although Peter thought he was having a dream it was really happening to him. They both passed by the guards and when they got to the city gate it opened up by itself.

The angel walked with Peter for a while and then left him alone. Suddenly Peter realized that it wasn't a dream at all; he was really standing outside and wasn't in jail anymore. Peter went to the house of Mary who was the mother of John and they had many people there praying for God to save Peter. When Peter knocked on the outer gate door a servant girl answered it and excitedly ran back to the house proclaiming that Peter was at the door.

Here these people were gathered together praying for Peter and when he knocks on the door they tell the servant girl she's out of her mind. Then when she kept insisting they said it must be his angel. Can you believe that? How could they be praying and when the answer came they didn't believe? Peter didn't give up though. He kept knocking and they finally opened the door. When they saw him they were astonished. Their prayers were answered! There was great rejoicing that night because God had shown His mighty hand.

Then Peter left to another place and the next morning when Herod found out about it he had the soldiers guarding Peter executed. This story is told in the book of Acts in chapter twelve and it always amazes me when I read it to see that when their prayers were answered the people still didn't believe. Stories like these made me chuckle silently as I sat in my own jail cell wondering if God would send an angel to deliver me. I wondered if I suddenly appeared in one of the churches where people were praying for me if they would think it was my angel and not really me. As I pondered these things I could hear commotion coming from around the cell area where I was imprisoned.

The headlines in some state newspapers read: "Saint David Disappears." Another newspaper headline read: "He saved others can he save himself?" My mother was devastated with despair over the whole ordeal and I could hear her now, "David, I told you not to go gallivanting all over across the world. You always were too independent, you need for Tracy to tie you down and keep you in line." Maybe she was right; I was so busy with my business and the cross that I never thought to stop my goal of preaching to the world the love of Jesus. *Oh well, maybe if I get out of here I will set a new course for my life and try to settle down more.* Isn't it funny that when a man is in trouble he starts to think about God, his wife and his mother? I guess we are all just trying to grow up in certain ways.

I'm not sure how many days at the time I was in that dark dungeon and my prayer life was all the more active than ever before. It's strange how when we seem close to maybe dying that nothing in our lives is important anymore. Things that we thought were the most important, like money and being successful, are now meaningless. I told God that I already had given Him my life so if He chose to take it that would be okay with me, the only thing I asked was that he took care of my family. I wondered why would God allowed this to happen to me when I was doing what He wanted me to do. It all didn't make sense in the overall scheme of what I was doing in Israel, which was taking the time to try to let them see that their Messiah had already come for them.

I prayed that God would take away the veil that covered the eyes of the Jewish people. I prayed that in whatever way He wanted to use me to help the people of Israel I was open to His will. But this, I wondered, how was this any help? Why I should be making speeches for the Jewish communities? Here I was suffering in a dark cell. I just knew my mother and Tracy were worried sick for me. Even though they would pray, still their instincts would make them worry. I figured out if it was day or night by what they gave me to eat. So I had already eaten a few hours ago and I suspected it must be around ten o'clock at night. I was lying on the dirt floor bundled up like an abandoned baby.

I remembered back to the time when Jesus was in great agony at the garden of Gethsemane and He asked His disciples to pray. His soul was overwhelmed at what was to come and the pain of being crucified and bearing the sins of the world. The disciples fell asleep and Jesus was in great sorrow; soon afterwards the guards came to arrest Him. At His most desperate time no one was there to give Him encouragement. I sometimes think if I could have been with Jesus during His lifetime I would never leave His side.

After several hours of not being able to sleep I saw a vision. I saw a small child walking through a minefield and I was yelling for the child to stand still. I could not move to go get him and he continued walking. Suddenly I was given wings to fly and I hovered above the child and brought him to safety. When he was safe in my arms I asked him what in the world he was doing walking in a minefield. He said he was wondering in the wilderness looking for his promised land. When I asked him how long he had been wondering out there he said for thousands of years. I asked why he never blew himself up in the minefield and he said because God was directing his steps. I asked him, if God was directing his steps, why did he not ever get to the promised land and he replied, "I didn't have enough faith for that."

Then he said to me, "Now you know where the mine fields are, go tell my brothers and sisters," and he disappeared.

I was awakened by my captures serving me food and I remembered the vision and pondered its meaning. There was a lot of commotion going on about around the place where I was being kept and I thought maybe I was in some kind of military camp. I heard the sound of a mighty rushing wind. Was God Almighty coming for me? I wondered. Within a few minutes my cell door burst open and I was stuck with some kind of needle in my arm. That's all I remember. A deep sound sleep came over me and I was knocked completely out.

What happened while I was knocked out was the Israeli Defense Forces had previously put a tracking device in my clothing without my knowledge and were making plans for my rescue. The reason they did not do it right away was they feared for my life and had to do the rescue at the precise time to save me. Helicopters flooded the area where I was being held and the soldiers stormed the terrorist camp. I was found and flown to a hospital just in case I was hurt. The Israeli soldiers who stormed the compound also found the largest cache of weaponry ever in the history of Israel. The weapons the terrorists had were enough to destroy the whole country of Israel. Had I not been kidnapped and taken hostage the weapons would not have been found. They also found plans on how the terrorists were going to go about this attack on a scale that was massive. The documents pointed the finger at some high-level individuals and countries that wanted the destruction of God's blessed nation. In fact it took weeks for Israel to get all the weaponry out of the compound.

When I realized that it was my signal that was sent to let Israel know where I was, I become conscious that this was the meaning of my vision I had in that dark dungeon. God had directed the steps of the Israeli government by my kidnapping to save their country from destruction. I marveled over the whole event, but my part in the ordeal was downplayed for reasons I cannot go into for security issues.

Since I'd found the cross I had been shot twice, crippled and now kidnapped. I thought about the Apostle Paul who said, "I have worked much harder, been in prison more frequently, been flogged more severely, and been exposed to death again and again. Five times I received from the Jews the forty lashes minus one. Three times I was beaten with rods, once I was stoned, three times I was shipwrecked, I spent a night and a day in open sea, I have been constantly on the move. I have been in danger from rivers, in danger from bandits, in danger from my own countrymen, in danger from Gentiles; in danger in city, in danger in country, in danger at sea; and in danger from false brothers. I have labored and toiled and have often gone with out sleep; I have known hunger and thirst and have often gone without food; I have been cold and naked. Besides everything else, I face daily the pressure of my own concern for all the churches" (2 Corinthians 11:23-28).

I guess I had really no excuse to complain when Paul, who was mighty in God, went through all this in his life and yet I was in distress over what I was going through! That humbled me to realize how much a person could go through for the gospel of Jesus and yet here I was extremely blessed and because I had to go through some trials I was worn out by it. "God," I prayed, "have mercy on me for being so shallow."

God was working powerfully in my life and delivered me in whatever situations I found myself. I felt embarrassed in front of God. He had paid my debt and I wanted comfort, the comfort that we have in America. How blessed we are to live in a country where all our needs are met. I needed to have my heart defragmented like our computers need to be cleaned up from all the garbage that we load into them. I thanked the Lord with all that was within me for His grace and mercy. My heart ached for Tracy and what she must be going through. I had never felt so much love for her and she was my one and only gift from God. I had not been home for a while now so I flew home the first chance I got.

# HOME AGAIN

It was great to be home again and I was greeted with a hero's welcome. Many millions of people prayed for my safe return and here I was back on the soil of America again. I was met with hundreds of fans at the airport that came to show their support for me. My greatest fan was my wife Tracy. When I first saw her beautiful eyes and long flowing hair, I knew I was totally blessed by my Heavenly Father. We hugged and I felt as though I never wanted to let her go. My body was shaking over the emotion I felt at that moment. Never before had I felt so much love for her as I did at that one precise moment. Mom and the children were there also and we had a nice family reunion. I signed autographs for the crowd and even gave a short speech to thank them for their prayers. Most of all, I wanted everybody to know that I felt my life was in God's hands all throughout the entire ordeal and I very much appreciated their prayers.

To go from a stinky underground cell back to my house was an incredible feeling. I took a long hot bath, which is what I do occasionally to relax. Tracy filled the tub with bubble bath I think she got from Michael. She even put in some plastic floating fish for fun. She always surprises me with little pleasures to make me feel like a child now and then. I put on some worship music and sunk down into the warmth of goodness. I thanked God that Israel had been spared a situation that could have brought a lot of devastation and death. How I loved God's land with all my heart and I am forever joined with the people there because of the cross of Jesus Christ. I prayed for the peace of Jerusalem and for safety of God's people. Tracy even put a full-sized beach towel out for me that read, "Welcome home, David."

Towards the evening I was exhausted and Michael wanted me to play with him so we made a puzzle together while baby Jean sat quietly watching. Mother was still visiting and helping Tracy with the kids, so we were all together at last and I was very happy. Mom asked how my legs were doing and I told her that each day it seemed they were stronger and I haven't had any problem walking at all. In fact it felt like I was never crippled.

# HEAL THE SICK, RAISE THE DEAD

The next day I was watching television with great interest as Daniel was getting ready to give a major speech. The speech was to be aired live worldwide. Tracy was out shopping with Mother, Michael and the baby. The speech was being translated in many different languages around the globe. Daniel stepped up to the podium and was giving a pretty interesting speech on his view of world politics. One of the stage hands working the event was seen coming up behind Daniel. Suddenly gunshots rang out in a burst of blasts that sounded like Fourth of July fireworks going off. The crowd went into frenzy, Daniel fell in a slump on the stage and everybody was running everywhere. Confusion rapidly took over the scene and it was chaos. The cameras turned away from the body that seemed to lay there lifeless.

My mind was instantly flashed back to the day that I had been shot and sprawled out on the ground. I will never forget the shots ringing out; sometimes at night I relive the event and jump in my sleep. The news coverage would not point the cameras back on Daniel while they tried to make some sense out of the situation. You could hear the commotion in the background though as the cameras rolled on. I had to shut the television off; it was bringing back haunting memories of what happened the day I was shot and it really bothered me.

Tracy and the gang walked into the living room and I told them what happened. We all were stunned and didn't know what to think about Daniel being shot. The tragedy became one of those stories where it dominates the news without interruption. Later on in the evening it was reported that Daniel was dead of a gunshot wound in the head. Many in the world mourned, just as deeply as the majority of the world did for Princess Diana. The next day thousands of flowers poured in from all over the globe with sincerest sympathy. The funeral was set to be in a few more days.

The very next day controversy raged as the Roman Empire announced they were trying to get a healing stick to give to Daniel. Using a healing stick on a person who had already died had never been tried before. We have seen many great healings take place all across the world, including legs growing back, cancer victims healed, and blind people being able to see again, but never had anyone tried something such as this before. It created a hurricane of controversy throughout the entire earth. Some said it was not right to intervene in matters relating to God. Others said why not, everyone else has tried healings sticks on everything imaginable; why not see if it works this time?

Into the second day after the assassination, the government of Rome was still trying to get its hands on a stick. I'm sure they could have gotten one by now but because of the great controversy over it they were weighing in on what to do. On day three the decision had been made; Daniel was going to be given a healing stick and the event would be filmed, but not televised. The world was about to find out for the first time since Jesus Christ if a man could be raised from the dead. Bible prophesy teachers went into high gear more than ever before, and what was foretold in the book of Revelation seemed to be coming to pass. The only thing that threw everybody off track was that if Daniel was really the Antichrist then why didn't the Rapture happen first? Nobody could figure this out; some said that Jesus would come right after the man of sin was revealed and if this was really the Antichrist then he would be raised from the dead and the Rapture would take place.

The Christian world was on the edge of its seat waiting to see the events unfold. Many people thought that this could not be the Antichrist. It just so happened that the healing sticks were found and why shouldn't they be used to bring a dead man back to life? Controversy flooded the land like the great flood waters of Noah's day.

Many talk show callers had their own insight into what was going on. One caller said that the healing sticks being found and used in this way was not Bible prophesy, it was just pure coincidence. Still other callers thought that God was able to do whatever He wanted because the order of things happening in Revelation didn't exactly have to happen in some kind of chronological order. Another caller said that in the book of Revelation in chapter thirteen when the beast rises up it also says, "This calls for patient endurance and faithfulness on the part of the saints" (Revelation13: 10). He thought that meant that we were allowed to see the rise of the beast before the rapture of the saints.

The talk show host read the following verse, "Since you have kept my command to endure patiently, I will also keep you from the hour of trial that is going to come upon the whole world to test those who live on the earth" (Revelation 3:10). This he believed meant that God would take the church before the Son of Perdition was revealed. Callers after that said the scripture applied to the unbelievers going through some kind of judgment, not the Church, and that was why it said He would keep us from that time. I myself had always believed in a pre-tribulation Rapture. To me the Bible makes that pretty clear, but at the same time I never limit God to my understanding of the scripture.

I got a call that day from my good Christian pastor from a great church in Israel. He said he understood that I wouldn't want to come back to Israel just yet after what I had gone through, but if I could he would be grateful if I could make a video tape giving my blessings to a massive group of God's servants who were raised up as a result of the great healings being done in Israel. I asked him if they were Christians and he told me they were all Jewish. He said many claimed to be from the Twelve Tribes and they were on fire for the word of God and the cities were in awe over this many Jewish people proclaiming that Jesus was indeed the Messiah. I asked him what church they attended and he laughed at the question. When I asked him why he laughed, he said, "There are probably around one hundred and fifty thousand of them and they could never fit into one church." My heart went into a flurry as I remembered the scripture in Revelation that said, "Then I heard the number of those who were sealed: 144,000 from all the tribes of Israel" (Revelation 7:4). I trembled and said back to him that the best I could do was make a video giving them my blessings and with that we agreed.

I was electrified after the call; quickly I looked up in the Bible in Matthew where it talks about the end times. I read, "For then there will be great distress, unequaled from the beginning of the world until now—and never to be equaled again. If those days had not been cut short, no one would survive, but for the sake of the elect those days will be shortened. At that time if anyone says to you, look, here is the Christ! Or, There he is! Do not believe it. For false Christ's and false prophets will appear and perform great signs and miracles to deceive even the elect—if that were possible. See, I have told you ahead of time" (Matthew 24:21-25). I wondered what it meant to us right now when it said if those days were not cut short. Many have read that over and over again, but here we were with the man many believed to be the Antichrist ready to be raised from the dead and now the 144,000 Jews were assembled and ready to proclaim their Messiah. What a time for the church to know whom they were and what was taking place before our very eyes.

My desk started shaking right under me and a great earthquake was happening right at the time I was reading this scripture. It only lasted a few minutes, but that was the first earthquake I was ever in. I had the radio on quietly and it came on as a news flash. It wasn't a huge damaging earthquake, but it rattled my nerves. Lately we had been witnessing tornadoes and hurricanes raging out of control. All the previous catastrophes that the world had had over the last few years were small in comparison to the events that had been taking place by Mother Nature.

I went into searching the word of God concerning what was going on and I came across this scripture that said, "The dragon gave the beast his power and his throne and great authority. One of the heads of the beast had a fatal wound, but the fatal wound had been healed. The whole world was astonished and followed the beast. Men worshipped the dragon because he had given authority to the beast, and they also worshipped the beast and asked, 'Who is like the beast? Who can make war against him?'" (Revelation 13:2-4). This was sending shivers through my spine. Was I the person, who by finding the cross, was responsible for bring life to the beast after he was shot in the head?

I dropped to my knees and cried out to the Lord in great anguish, "Dear Lord Jesus," I prayed, "am I responsible for bringing this King of Babylon back from the dead? Have I been led astray only to be used by Satan? Father, if I am out of your will, may you have mercy on me forever." I sobbed uncontrollably. The answer from God came back to me with astounding strength and I heard the voice of God speak boldly unto me.

"My son, you have found favor before the Lord your God. All these things must take place on the earth. I have chosen you as my servant to do as I have commanded and you have obeyed without hesitation. Great is your reward for my word has been found deep within your heart. Be of good cheer, my child, and walk in peace knowing that my will be done!"

I was encased with love and peace from on high. I was so distraught after reading about the beast being shot in the head and coming back to life that I thought my heart would burst. It was only the comfort of the Holy Spirit that brought supernatural peace to me to allow me to go on in God's will.


## LET GOD BE PRAISED

I took on even more celebrity status because of my kidnapping, everybody wanted to interview me. I did do some interviews and told the public I needed a rest from everything and so I was taking a vacation to have some quiet relaxation. My time with family and friends would be just what I needed. The world scene had gotten somewhat nuttier though. Daniel still had not been given a healing stick and I wondered how long they were going to wait. Maybe they thought the longer he was dead the more people would worship him if he came back to life. I wondered if by now they would even still try, seeing it had already been days since he died.

There were more terrorist attacks around the world. New diseases had come about and weather patterns were causing storms that filled people's hearts with terror. It almost seemed like the time was prophetic in nature. God's healings were being poured out and the earth seemed like it was going through birth pains, reeling to and fro. The whole reaction to the healing sticks worldwide was still being felt the world over. It seemed like the wooden sticks from the cross of Jesus Christ, the Savior of the world, were what ushered in the last and incredible time of the greatest revival the Church had ever seen.

Stories and testimonies aired on national television showing groups of people in hospitals being healed when only one person had a stick. God poured out His Spirit on countless millions of people worldwide and showed His mercy by healing many millions more people than the sticks could have ever healed. Even though the world still had all the same problems and was reeling like a drunkard, it seemed a better place to live because God was headline news.

What was unusual was that people whose hearts were not open to the gospel just went their way as usual; they never even blinked. In nations where religion was not so open, persecution still existed. What did happen though is that there was a mighty outpouring of God's spirit over the planet earth as never before. Because of Israel giving the surrounding Muslim nations some healing sticks, they were experiencing a great explosion of revival too. The haters who wanted more sticks to mock Israel quieted down. Many Muslim people felt let down by their governments and because they saw the healings taking place, they were coming to God in great numbers. It was God calling the people back unto Himself.

Some countries were turned upside down by the gospel because things that they saw were very powerful. This caused a stir for religious leaders, but there was nothing they could do to stop the light of the gospel from coming to them like the flood waters that Moses parted. I was astounded that revival was coming to the Muslim nations so strong and it came in such a powerful and supernatural way. Many Muslims expected that Jesus would return and bring peace in a great time of trouble. They were teaching that He would be a just judge that would come to help the people of the earth. Many thought Jesus was a sign and they believed the day was coming for judgment. Although they held beliefs that are contrary to the Bible, a revival was causing millions to believe and come to Jesus. Ishmael was returning home and the homecoming was awe-inspiring. It goes to show that God was calling whosoever will to come home to Him in those final hours.

Nothing could stop this great number of people from coming to God, and relations between the Muslim nations and Israel started to get better. New friendships were forming and at last it seemed that peace was on the horizon. Although the terrorist activity increased, it was to only try to stop this great revival from happening. It was the terrorists last-ditch effort to throw a wrench in what God was doing. God had reached into the far corners of the earth and the gospel seemed to have been preached to every human on the planet. It was just a great time to be alive on the planet Earth. I was being refreshed in spite of the overwhelming things that had taken place in my life over the last few years. Our family was extremely close knit, as was the Church, for we all felt that our time of departure was at hand.

The Roman Empire was going to announce that they decided to bestow a healing stick to Daniel. The news stunned the church and many were beginning to gather in churches and not wanting to leave. God was still using the television industry to preach His gospel and it was full and complete with prophesies written thousands of years ago being talked about for all to see. It was almost as though if you didn't know what was going on and couldn't relate it to what we were now going through, then you as a person were without excuse. I thought about what Paul said in the book of Romans, "For since the creation of the world God's invisible qualities—his eternal power and divine nature—have been clearly seen, being understood from what has been made, so that men are without excuse" (Romans 1: 20).

Speculation of what Daniel would do if he were resurrected from the dead abounded everywhere. Would he be the man that took the Invisible Money idea and implemented it? Would the mark of the beast be the computer chip that was already being injected into some children whose parents thought they were looking after their best interest? The Man of Sin breaks the covenants that he makes with the Jewish people at the midpoint of the tribulation period by demanding that they worship him as God. This is revealed in book of Matthew, "So when you see standing in the holy place 'the abomination that causes desolation,' spoken of through the prophet Daniel—let the reader understand" (Matthew 24:15). Paul clarified this when he said, "He will oppose and will exalt himself over everything that is called God or is worshipped, so that he sets himself up in God's temple, proclaiming himself to be God" (2 Thessalonians 2:4).

Daniel had previously set up offices in Jerusalem. If he were to rise again, would he display all kinds of miracles, signs and wonders to deceive the masses as foretold in second Thessalonians chapter two? I didn't want to be around to see any of what was ahead. Tracy and I held onto our strong belief that God would keep us from this hour and the Rapture of the Church would be before the great tribulation period started.

News from Israel spread like Mount Saint Helens erupting. Two witnesses came on the scene and were becoming very well-known for prophesying and their interpretation of why God sent the healing sticks for the world at this time in history. Like strong winds of tornadoes, they spoke with boldness and gave all glory to Jesus the Messiah whom they claimed they served. Many likened them to Elijah and Moses. To us it was yet another sign that God was bringing about His word and fulfilling biblical prophesy. We didn't know when the coming of the Lord would be, but we did know the signs of the times. The Bible says that just like in Noah's days people ate and drank, they were married and they were divorced. But when Noah entered the Ark the people were swept away and that is how it will be when Jesus comes. Thankfully for the world's sake, God brought the most overwhelmingly, greatest revival we could have all hoped for. Never in any of God's chosen people did anybody think that such a revival was possible or likely before the coming of our Lord Jesus. God showed His kindness and mercy by giving the world one last chance to see His glory. For all to see that He holds the world close to His heart and does not wish for any person to perish without the chance of knowing that their names are written in the Lamb's Book of Life.

# EVEN SO COME LORD JESUS

The Bible talks about when Jesus returns for His church that two men will be working in a field and one of them will be taken. Two women will be grinding and one of them will be taken home, because of this you need to keep watch because you don't know the hour in which the Lord is coming.

Tracy and our family stood by these words and lived by the comfort of knowing that our eternal destiny was in the hands of a loving and forgiving Father. We knew that our sins were taken away by the blood that Jesus shed on the cross. This blood was so overpowering that just soaking into the wood of the cross two thousand years later the earth would experience the magnitude of healings as a result of what Jesus accomplished on that day of calvary. When He hung on the cross on the wood between heaven and earth our sins were forever taken away and a New Covenant was established. God had come into my life and given me the most wonderful experience I could have ever imagined and to top it off He gave me the love of a kind women and great children. I could not have asked for more and my heart still beats madly in love with my Lord Jesus.

The twenty-four elders up in heaven sang a new song to the Lamb that was slain singing, "You are worthy to take the scroll and to open its seals, because you were slain, and with your blood you purchased men for God from every tribe and language and people and nation. You have made them to be a kingdom and priests to serve our God, and they will reign on the earth" (Revelation 5:9,10).

I could hear the door hinges up in heaven getting ready to open wide the gates of splendor. At night we went to sleep as though it could be our last. The church was white and spotless and ready to go, the saints were washed clean by the blood of the Lamb. Television news acknowledged that there was a supernatural event getting ready to take place. Everybody felt it and God's praise was lifted beyond our wildest imaginations. It was a triumphant time to rest in God's love and the knowledge that we were going home.

I still had the dust that was collected from the cutting up of the cross under strict lock and key. Our experiments with the dust turned out that they did not hold any healing powers and so it was kept in security until I thought about what to do with it. I knew that someday God would tell me what to do with the dust in His own time. I was humbled when a top Israeli government official came to see me and told me that the government of Israel was planning on building a temple in Israel and wanted permission to take the dust so they could mix it in with the mortar for the building of the new temple in Jerusalem. They wanted the dust in recognition for all the wonderful healings that had taken place in their nation. After prayer and peace from God, I gave the dust of the cross to the country of Israel for this project. Somehow it seemed appropriate that my name is David and I had a part in the rebuilding of the new temple.

Signs of the times were definitely abundant and the masses of God's children were aware of them. The Bible says: "For the Lord Himself will come down from heaven, with a loud command, with the voice of the archangel and with the trumpet call of God, and the dead in Christ will rise first. After that, we who are still alive and are left will be caught up together with them in the clouds to meet the Lord in the air" (1 Thessalonians 4:16,17).

Also, the Bible says: "But you, brothers, are not in darkness so that this day should surprise you like a thief" (1 Thessalonians 5:4,5). This "Rapture" the Bible was talking about was at the very door and we all knew it. Daniel had been given a healing stick and the Roman Empire was scheduled to have a worldwide announcement to tell the people now what took place. Nobody knew if he was dead or alive and we realized that the answer to that question would determine our fate. The world waited in suspense for the coming announcement.

The world scene was given the most wonderful and spectacular revival in its history. You could look up in the clouds and almost see the trumpets ready to sound. The signs were here and Christians waited with eager expectations. The Church was in its finest hour indeed and God was on the minds of almost everyone. The church of Jesus beamed in His glory as the love of God shined across the world in illuminating manner. The clouds above seemed to shout out the words of John when he revealed, "The Spirit and the bride say, 'Come!' And let him who hears say, 'Come!' Whoever is thirsty, let him come; and whoever wishes, let him take the free gift of the water of life" (Revelation 22:17). Jesus was standing at the door knocking on the hearts of every man, woman, and child and the response was miraculous. It was very common for folks to say as they were parting, in each their own language to one another from around the globe, "If Jesus comes today I'll see you in heaven!"

Maranatha.

# Testimony

After I received my Associates degree and another degree in the mail and I was going to buy a couple of frames for the two degrees. For the last month, I had been looking for my "new birth certificate" that had the date I prayed and asked Jesus to come into my heart. I couldn't remember the exact date that I prayed this for the first time so many years ago, and so I wanted to find the certificate and buy three frames all at once. When searching through some old stuff of mine it fell out of an old photograph book I was looking through. On August 23, 2003, I went to the store and bought three frames and hung them in my office room.

I received the book contract in the mail from PublishAmerica on June 25 for my new book *Healing Sticks* and had people look over the publisher's contract to see if I should sign it. When I got the okay from knowledgeable people to sign the contract, I signed it and mailed it to the publisher on June 30, 2003.

I always write important dates in my calendar so each year I have everybody's birthdays, and so I can remember important things. That night I couldn't sleep; I tossed and turned just thinking about the calendar for some peculiar reason. The next day, with my "new birth certificate" in hand, I went to write down on my calendar under June 30, that I had prayed to receive Jesus on that day, 28 years ago. I was taken by surprise at what I wrote down in the calendar. It was now 55 days later that I wrote in the calendar on June 30 and it was the very day that I signed the book contract for *Healing Sticks*! That is exactly 28 years to the very day that I was saved at a Doug Clark Amazing Prophesy Rally in Phoenix, Arizona, after watching a movie called *Burning Hell*. I went into my filing cabinet to look at the post office receipts and, sure enough, there was that date: June 30.

Tears came into my eyes as I honored it as a gift from God to me. He took my dreams and made them into a reality because He is faithful and kind. I love Jesus for showing Himself to me in such a real way as He did that day.

Why is this so important to me now, after seeing time line up so strategically? Because I could have mailed in that contract any day, there was no time limit for me to sign it. Also, this was before I found my new birth certificate, so I wasn't aware of the exact day I was saved. I had no idea of a date for anything; I was just going about my everyday business. So for me to see that God moved in my life in such a way 28 years later to the very day was His way of showing me that He loved me and cares!

Now I don't know how successful the book will be, because as an unknown author it is difficult to draw attention to the book. I believe that God will make the book a great success and I am hoping a Christian ministry will make the book into a movie. I also want to give you the opportunity to get to know the Jesus in this book, who is so loving and kind. If you would like to accept God's offer of salvation, please pray this prayer and I believe God is faithful and will give you eternal life:

> Dear Lord Jesus, I thank You for dying for the forgiveness of my sins. I want to receive your righteousness and your resurrected life. I accept you and Your gift of salvation. I ask You to guide me and live your life through me each and every day. Thank You for your grace and the new life you have now given me. I pray this prayer to you in your wonderful name.

I encourage you to start reading the New Testament and to continue to seek God every day. He will make Himself known to you. May God richly bless you and keep you now and forever!

# Notes

*For readers who would like to look up*
*certain scriptures and write about them.*